Another
Different
Life

Another Different Life

. . .

Marisa Kantor Stark

For information address Warner Books, 1271 Avenue of the Americas, New York, NY 10020.

W A Time Warner Company

ISBN 0-7595-5008-5

First edition: April 2001

Visit our Web site at www.iPublish.com

C O N T E N T S

CONTENTS

CHAPTER 1

When I come home tonight, I know right away there's trouble. Just walking up the steps, I feel it on my face. I'm coming from picking up the baby at the neighbor. She is very heavy lying on my arm. Very hot. She sticks to my skin. The sign by the bank says one hundred.

In my other arm I'm carrying the books. They're from the Adult Education Center, where I go once a week after work to learn English. She gave them to me because I failed the test. You had to get twenty-five right, and I only got twenty-four. She said read, read, study the verbs, and when you're ready you can take the test again. But I have some problems with this language. It's not easy for me. My own language is Spanish.

All I want is to get to my apartment and put everything down. I want a glass of cranberry juice with ice. I don't want trouble. I don't need more trouble.

The steps to my apartment are very narrow. You can't even get a carriage up. I always have to leave it downstairs inside the door and pray to myself nobody takes it. It's a good carriage that Eddie bought, not a piece of junk. I don't know why they didn't take it yet. Every time I leave it there, I think I'll never see it again.

It is past suppertime. I can smell the leftovers from everyone's meal. Fried meat, onions. All the smells get trapped on the steps. You can know what people had for supper when you come downstairs the next morning.

And you can hear everything. You hear them banging their pans against the stove and their babies crying and the TVs going in the kitchen even when there's nobody there to watch. Upstairs from my apartment, I hear noise like someone throwing furniture. It can happen anytime, even the middle of the night. I told Eddie the man up there beats his wife. He is very polite when you meet him on the stairs. He always smiles and says good morning. But like I told Eddie, that doesn't mean anything. Eddie said it's none of our business what they do.

I come to the third floor to my apartment. Now the feeling is very strong. I don't want to go in. I'm sick in the stomach just thinking about going in there. But I don't know another way. When you live somewhere and you get there, you go inside. Also Shyla is starting to cry. She wants her food. She's always hungry, that baby.

I stand for one second listening by the door. I don't hear anything. Maybe I'm wrong, I think. Please God, let me be wrong.

There are two locks on my door, with two keys. Eddie,

who is the super for the building, put them there. I do one lock and then the other one and try to push open the door. It makes some noise, but it won't open. It's stuck again. How many times did I tell Eddie fix this door, but he says he can't fix it. It's wood, he says, and wood gets stuck in the summer. So I'm standing there, and I can't even get into my own apartment.

Shyla is really crying. Her face is red and wrinkled. Why doesn't she shut up? I think. She's ugly when she cries. I shake her up and down. With my shoulder I push against the door. One of the books slides out from my arms and falls on my toe. I can't bend down to get it. Shit, I say.

It is very hot in the hallway. The heat is like a thousand needles on my face and arms.

Shut your mouth, I say to Shyla, and I shake her harder. She starts screaming. I think to myself I could kill this baby.

Then the door opens from the inside and he is there.

I came back, he says in English.

C H A P T E R

2

Three days ago I came home from work and the phone was ringing. I heard it when I was still outside the door, and I thought I can't get my key out fast enough, so I won't even try. Whoever is there will call again. But it kept ringing and ringing. Damn, I said. Don't they ever stop? I got into the apartment and picked it up. It was my brother Carlos, in California.

I lost Ricky, he said.

I laughed. Not a real laugh, just a dry noise inside my throat.

No, really. He's gone. He didn't come home last night at all.

What do you mean he's gone? Where is he?

I don't know. He took the bicycle, and my cellular phone.

He said at first he didn't realize it, because he works very late and when he came home he thought Ricky was already in bed. And his wife, Lisa, thought he came in after she went to sleep. It was only tonight they realized he wasn't in the house. They looked in the side room, where he was staying, and his bed was neat like he never slept there. The cellular phone in the hall was missing.

I just stood, holding the receiver to my ear. But where is he? I kept saying.

I told you, I don't know, Carlos said. All I know is he's not here.

Lisa got on the phone. We'll call the police, she said. They'll find him.

No, Carlos said. He'll come back. Where else would he go? He doesn't know anyone in California.

Let him go, I said.

What? Lisa said.

I said let him go. Louder, so she would hear.

You can't do that.

Why not?

He's just a kid. If he was my kid—

He's not your kid.

Wait a little longer, Carlos said. I say he'll come back here.

I don't care where he goes, I said.

I am not the keeper for my son.

CHAPTER

3

When I told him some weeks ago I'm sending you to California, he didn't want to go.

Why? I said. It's nice in California. They grow oranges.

I live here now.

Salado. I had enough of you here. Maybe you'll learn something over there.

Please. Give me one more chance.

I'd never heard him ask for something. I almost changed my mind.

But I knew how it was. I wouldn't make that kind of mistake. No, I said. No more chances.

He said I won't go, you can't make me go, but I said if you won't go I'll have Carlos come and get you. He will tie you up and put you on that plane.

Fuck you, he said.

On the morning he was supposed to leave he took a

long time getting ready. I stood by the curtain to his room.

Hurry up, we'll be late.

I'm looking for something, he said. He was moving things around in his bag.

What are you looking for?

It's not your business.

We'll be late. You'll miss the plane.

I'm not going until I find it.

I watched him throw things out of the bag onto the floor. Shirts, socks, Nintendo, gum. I didn't know what to do. He had to go. If he didn't go I couldn't live another day. I went into my own room and grabbed some money from the money box. Here, I said. Whatever it is, you can buy another one. There's stores in California.

He looked up at me, then away. I can see he is surprised. I don't give him money.

I don't need your fucking money, he said. But he didn't give it back to me. He zipped up the bag.

Thank God, I thought.

We took a taxi to the airport. There was traffic. Can you drive faster, can you go a different way? I said to the taxi man.

I can't fly, he said.

We were late. The man at the desk said the gate is already closed.

Please, I said. He has to be on this plane.

I'm sorry, lady, he said. Takeoff is in four minutes.

He has just this one bag, I said.

There's other planes later today. He can go standby.

I don't understand standby. But I know it means Ricky will not go now to California.

No. He has to go now. Now.

He looked at me closely. Is this some kind of emergency?

Yes, I said. I pay my money. I need my son to get on this plane.

Okay, he said. I'll see what I can do. He picked up a red phone on his desk.

Gate thirteen, he said. You better run.

I ran. Ricky wouldn't run. When I came to the gate I told them he's coming, he's coming, just wait.

Don't worry, the woman said. She had short dark hair and a pretty smile. We have programs for kids traveling alone. We'll look after him.

You hear? I said to Ricky. They'll be watching you.

He went without looking back.

My legs were shaking. I stood by a wall that was all glass and watched his plane disappear into the night. I leaned my cheek against the glass.

Finally, I thought. I can have my own life back again.

•   •   •

Ten months he was living here. He went places, did things, I never knew what. He liked to go look at cars. I told him Ricky, you get a job in the summer, make some money, but he didn't care about this. He didn't listen to anything I told him. When he was in the apartment, he sat and played Nintendo. Where did you get all this Nintendo? I said. I borrowed it, he said, not looking at me. He never looked at the person when they talked to him.

I used to call the police and ask them to come. Please, *señor*, I said. Please come here and take my boy.

What did he do? the man said the first time I called.

He's no good. He won't listen to nothing.

This is a police station, not a reform school.

The next week I called again. Please take him, I said.

Listen, he said. You can't keep calling here. You gotta handle your own things.

He's very big, I said.

Are you being threatened? Are you in physical danger?

Cómo? What did you say?

Did he hit you?

No.

We can't do anything, then. We can't do anything unless there's actual violence.

So I stopped calling.

Eddie said he's dangerous. He can hurt someone, maybe hurt the baby. But I said no. He's crazy, but he's not dangerous. Once he raised his hand to me, but he didn't hit me. He never hit me. He wouldn't hurt anyone.

That's what you say, Eddie said.

Before he came here, he lived with my mother and my other son in Costa Rica. Then she called one Saturday morning when I was getting ready for church. It was early, not even eight o'clock yet. And it was one hour earlier over there. But my mother always got up early.

I don't work Saturdays. I'm a Seventh Day Adventist. My family is not. They are Catholic. My father was very Catholic. He gave a lot of money to the church so that when he died he could go to heaven. When I was a little girl, I went with him to that church. It was a white building on a hill. Inside it smelled like wood and wax from the candles. I sat between my brothers on the bench, very still. I stared at the face of the Virgin Mary in the colored glass over the altar. She had kind brown eyes. I didn't swing my feet because he hated if you did that. We went every Sunday. But when I came to this country I changed.

I was ironing my blue dress with the white dots. Saturday is the only day I get dressed. Other days to work I wear shorts and a T-shirt or Eddie's old undershirt. I don't care too much how I look. But Saturday is different. I try to look nice. I spread the dress on the kitchen counter and put water and a measure of salt in the iron. When I'm at home, I don't feel like taking out the ironing board.

When the phone rang, I thought it was my friend Jackie. Sometimes she calls and we go to church together. Eddie doesn't go. He doesn't have religion. I told him that's okay. Saturday is my day. You do what you do, I'll do what I do. You have to feel your religion. He stays in his own apartment and watches TV, or he works on something in the basement. He has his tools down there. He was making a toy box for the baby.

But it wasn't Jackie calling.

I'm sending Ricky to you, my mother said. She didn't even say how are you.

What happened? I said.

Nothing happened, she said.

It's hard to talk on the phone to Costa Rica. The call doesn't reach, or it hangs up in the middle. Many times the connection is not so good. You say something and there's a long wait before she hears you. Then you start to talk again, but she starts to answer what you said before, and both people are talking. That's why I didn't call there so often, because it's hard to talk. Sometimes I talked to her. Sometimes I talked to the boys. I'd ask them how are you and they said fine.

Are you being good boys?

Yes.

You be good now.

Maybe once a month I talked to them. Is that Ricky or Miguel? I said. I could never tell which one unless I asked. If it was Ricky I said you take care of your brother. Because Ricky is two years older. It's almost exactly two years. He was born at the end of February, and Miguel was born the beginning of March. I remember when I was pregnant with Miguel. I thought won't it be funny if this second one is born the same day as the first. Out of all the days in the year. I thought about it so much I started to believe that was how it would be. They'll have one birthday, like twins. But of course it didn't happen that way. It never happens how you think.

I'm too old to take care of two boys, my mother said.

I left the iron too long on the dress. There was a hissing sound and the smell of material burning.

Shit, I said. I leaned against the counter. You know, I'm pregnant.

You never learn, do you? she said.

Please, Mama. A little longer. The baby's coming next month. I'll send you more money.

No, she said. Already it's been long enough.

How much? How much do you want?

I don't want anything. I'll keep one. Miguel I'll keep here with me.

What's wrong with Ricky?

Nothing, she said. If I need help to move something around the house, he helps me move it.

Then why?

I told you. And I have a weak knee.

You always had a weak knee.

I got him a visa. He's coming on the twelfth.

She hung up. I tried to call her back. I let the phone ring maybe thirty times, but she didn't pick up.

I didn't feel like going to church anymore. I could still smell the burnt material from my dress. I felt a little bit sick. Maybe I'm going to throw up, I thought, even though I didn't throw up since the first month I was pregnant. I went into the bathroom and leaned over the toilet. Nothing happened.

The phone rang again. I was hoping maybe she'd call back. But this time it was Jackie. I'll stop by to pick you up, she said.

I'm not ready, I said.

Is something wrong? You're never late for church.

No, I said. I'll meet you there.

I forced myself to get dressed. The dress had a small brown burn under the arm, but I had no choice except to wear it. I don't have another one. I thought I won't pick up my arm and nobody will see. Anyway, they're supposed to pray, not look at what other people are wearing.

The church was crowded, and I didn't look for Jackie. I sat in the back by myself. I closed my eyes and prayed about Ricky. Please God, let him be nice, I said.

It was three years since I saw him. I didn't want him here. I had another different life.

• • •

I came to this country after my father died. I stood on the hill by the church and watched them put him into the ground, and I said to myself I will go to America. Carlos said if you're coming at least come here to California, but I said no, I want to start my own life. I wanted to go to New York, but it was too expensive to live, so I came to New Jersey. Carlos knew some people here and they let me stay with them while I looked for work. I came to work.

I got a visa for six months. With a travel visa you can go back and forth in the country, but you can't work. But I broke the rules. It wasn't too bad what I did. If I work here I can make a lot more money than if I work over there. In my country the economy is not so good. Most people are poor. One percent or two percent of the people have all the money. My father had money. He had a big house with many rooms. Some of the rooms even had a carpet. But after I left his house I didn't take anything from him. I knew how to work. Before I came here, I worked in a store for an old man who was blind. I sold food and wine.

Here I work for a lot of different people. I clean houses. I have friends who know people.

I like my job. I like to clean. To cook, no, I hate to cook, but I love to clean. I take someplace that is dirty and make it new again. When I come to the house, the first thing I do is take off my shoes and leave them by the door, like we did in Costa Rica. Then I start at the top of the house and go down through the rooms. I prefer when there is nobody home. This way there's nobody to mess up what I do, to step on the wet floor or bring dirt on the rug. When I close the door on the house, everything is perfect. The last thing I see before I leave is a perfect house, and this is the picture I keep with me until I come back again the next week. Sometimes if I'm by myself I make a cup of coffee and put on some music. The Spanish station. At the school she says listen to English radio and television, it's the best way to pick up the language. But when I'm working I listen to what I like.

If the woman is at home I stop work to talk to her. They like to talk. They tell me about their husbands or their children. This one is taking ballet lessons, this one is going to college. Maybe I don't understand everything, but I smile like I understand. They ask me how is your baby? How old is she now?

Nine months, I say.

Is she walking?

Nah, she's not walking yet. She doesn't like to walk. I say Shyla come and I put out my hands. So maybe she's taking a little step.

When Ricky came, they started asking also about him. So how does your son like America?

He doesn't like anything, I said. He doesn't like me also.

Oh, come on now. I'm sure that's not true.

I think he's crazy, I'd say. *Loco,* crazy.

I'd make the sign for crazy by my head, and the woman would laugh. She thought maybe I was making a joke. But it wasn't a joke.

• • •

That morning in the church I didn't realize, but I was praying a long time. When I opened my eyes, people were already leaving. I walked home together with Jackie. She lives in the same building.

My son is coming from Costa Rica, I told her.

You're lucky it's a boy, she said. Girls can be trouble.

Jackie has two daughters.

I don't know, I said.

Yes, she said. With the girls, there's all kinds of problems. You understand what I'm saying?

She asked me do I want to come to her apartment for coffee. Sometimes we sit together after church and talk, maybe listen to some music. Or Jackie polishes her nails. After she polishes them, she holds her fingers very stiff. She works in the post office, and she keeps her hands nice. Smooth skin, oval nails like perfect eggs. Not like me. My skin has little cracks and my nails are always short and broken. When they break, I peel them. You can't clean houses and have pretty hands. Some women wear gloves to clean, but I don't like this. I like to touch things and to feel what I'm touching.

It's nice visiting Jackie. There's no place to go, nothing to do. In my country people also visit like that, one to the other. But that day I said no, I'm not feeling so great. I think today I'll just go home.

When I got to my apartment, I went into the bedroom and opened the closet. On the top shelf was a fat glass fishbowl where I kept things. I had my money there and my postcards. I collect postcards from different places. If a woman I'm cleaning for goes on a vacation, I always ask her to send me a postcard. I have Paris, Vienna, Istanbul, Jerusalem, all over the world. Because I'll never go to those places myself. I just go to work and home and that's all.

Also in that fishbowl was a picture of my sons. I hadn't taken it out in a very long time, but I knew it was there. I emptied the bowl on the floor to find it.

They don't look the same. They have different fathers. Ricky is darker and bigger. When he was born, he was almost nine pounds. It was a heavy nine pounds. They said how can someone so little carry such a big baby? He was born with his top lip cut in two halves, and they had to sew it together. You can still see the mark there.

Miguel has skin that's light, like wheat, and his face is pretty like a girl's. He's a lot smaller than Ricky. His bones are smaller. If I used to walk with them on the street, you couldn't tell they're brothers. I wondered how the new baby will be. Eddie has reddish hair and some freckles. He's not so big, but he's not so thin either.

I sat on the floor. The picture was taken a short time before I left Costa Rica. Ricky was ten. Now he's almost fourteen. He must look very different. They change very fast.

What will he say? What will I say? I don't know what food he likes to eat. It was too much. I felt my new baby moving around inside me. I didn't want him to come.

When I first came to this country, if I saw a boy walking or going with Rollerblades, I thought that could be Ricky, or that could be my little one, Miguel. And I felt something inside me, like a small piece of me was breaking off. It would slide around in there, and if I walked I walked slow, and if I talked I talked soft, so it wouldn't hurt. But still I felt the sharp edges poking my stomach, my lungs, my heart. Sometimes it was an hour, sometimes a whole day. But then the weeks passed and the months and I stopped feeling it. A boy on the street was just a boy, and that was all. I walked past him and nothing happened.

I looked again at the picture. Ricky is not looking at the camera. He hated for you to take his picture because of his lip. It's pulled up a little bit on the left side. It makes his mouth look like a heart. He always thought people were looking at him, staring at his lip. I told him nobody can notice it, but he didn't listen to me.

So I thought to myself I will know him by his lip. In Costa Rica they used to say it's where an angel pressed a finger before he was born. Some people said it is a blessing. Some people said it is a curse.

4

In Costa Rica I grew up near the beach. My father had a farm not very far from there, and when I was young if I had a few minutes I'd go there. Sometimes my father would say all right, you can play now. He gave us fifteen minutes to play, maybe twenty. Then you had to go back to work.

I used to get up at four or five o'clock to make food for the men on the farm. They liked to eat meat. *Casado,* meat married to rice, beans, and cabbage. In Costa Rica you cook a lot of rice and corn and potatoes. Everything is very fresh. You can't compare it to this country. Here you can forget what it smells like to have new grass growing, or tomatoes. The first time I went to the supermarket in this country, I wanted to buy some corn. But I could only find corn in a can or in a bag. I won't buy this. I'm used to having fresh corn. My father grew it on the farm. We let it dry out in the barn and then I took the kernels off the cob to grind flour. I mixed it with water to make tortillas.

It was still dark when I got up to make the food. I made a wood fire in the stove. I know how to make a fire. You have to cross the pieces with each other and weave the cracks with strips of paper. It's a special skill. If you don't do it exactly right, the flame goes out and you're left with only a dull blue glow inside the wood. Not everyone can do it, but I can do it. There was a stack of wood and paper by the stove.

The heat from the fire rolled across the floor in the kitchen and rose up like a fog into the air. Outside the window was a white moon. I used to think the world was moving to the moon, and someday it would get there. I cooked the tortillas and watched the sky around the moon get lighter, and I thought to myself we're coming closer and closer. Then the moon disappeared and became part of the sky, and I knew today wasn't the day it would happen. My father would come into the kitchen to check on me. He counted the tortillas. These are hungry men, he said. They work hard, they need to eat.

The only person was me. There was no one helping me. My brothers had other chores, the chickens and the pigs. My mother lived in a different town. One day my father took me and my brothers and moved us away from the town and the relatives in the town to live on this farm. It was very beautiful. Everything is green and wherever you look there's a little church poking up. Costa Rica is a beautiful country. It's in the middle, so we have birds from the north and birds from the south. The windows are open and they fly into the houses. And butterflies. Seventy percent of the world's butterflies are in Costa Rica. A lot of tourists come there. The temperature is eighty or ninety all year. They come to see the nature and the rain forests. You have to put on big rubber boots, then they take you into the forests. You can see monkeys and jaguars there.

The men ate their breakfast at the long wooden table in the kitchen. I went back and forth from the table to the stove with the food. They didn't talk a lot. They just ate, big plates of food for every man.

I kept the fire burning. When it went down, I poked it and the wood came alive again with hundreds of sparks. The smoky smell was always in my hair.

After they finished, they left the plates there and went out to the farm. Small birds came in and sat on the table to eat the crumbs. We called them the crumb-gathering birds. I cleaned the table. If there was something left, I ate. If no, no. I never ate very much. Then I got ready for school.

I walked with my brothers three miles to the school. Some of the roads are very bad. There were rocks, and they got in your shoes and cut your feet. During the rainy time, the road turns to mud and your feet get stuck there. Sometimes we met another child walking. In my country it's like here. They want you to go to school. In some families they don't care about it. If it's not good for them to go to school, they don't have to go. If their parents are busy on the farm, they stay home and help. But in my father's house you had to go to church, and you had to go to school. I went until the eighth grade.

My older brothers complained, but I didn't care. I liked school. I liked to sit at the desks with the other children and read from the books. It was a small wooden schoolhouse, light blue with a red door. We were all together in one room. At noon we had a break, and we could play with a ball in the dirt yard. Then later we walked the three miles home again. When we came home, we worked some more. I cooked the supper, cleaned the house, washed the clothes. My father said you have to do this, you have to eat this.

If you were sick, the teacher sent you home early. I used to hold the sneeze inside my mouth so she wouldn't send me. I learned how to keep it there, a tickle against the back of my throat, until I could go outside and let it out. I wanted to stay in school until the last minute. She rang a bell on her desk. The bell was shaped like an upside-down boat, and she hit it with a little stick.

At night I studied. After everyone went to bed and the house was quiet, I sat at the kitchen table with my books. My father's dog, Arsenio, would stay with me. He was very old. So old he forgot how to lie down. He would stand there one or two hours until you pushed his legs to make him go down. Sometimes he'd fall over. But after you put him down, he would stay lying. He was good company to me.

It wasn't easy. Sometimes I was so tired I couldn't see anything. I had to stop to sleep. But then I'd have to get up earlier in the morning to do it. Because you had to study. You couldn't get any grade under eighty. If you brought home a grade under eighty, he would beat you. He had a leather belt. I'm not raising children to be idiots, he said. He never went to school himself.

I'd tell myself you have to wake up at three o'clock, and I would wake up. I can do that.

One time I was studying in the middle of the night, and I heard a noise. In Costa Rica where we lived you didn't have to be afraid at night. People don't have locks on their door or a chain, like I have on my apartment. Some of them don't even have a key. We had a key hanging from a string on an old red nail by the door, but we never used it. People came in and out. It's not like here where you have to make an appointment to see someone. You just walk in. You can be there eating and someone comes to the door. *Upe!* they call through the door, instead of knocking. I never heard of anything happening, a robbery or something like that.

But it was very late. I didn't know who it would be.

Then I saw it was my father. He came into the kitchen. He had a short robe that was open at the top. I could see the black hair like curled wire on his chest. First he didn't see me. It was dark, and I had only one small light to read.

Arsenio? he called softly.

He's here, I said.

He turned. What are you doing up? he said.

I'm studying. I have a test.

Oh, he said. Good.

He went to the sink and filled a bowl with water. He bent down to where the dog was lying and gave him the water. He held Arsenio's head up while he drank.

It's a hot night, my father said. He can't drink by himself.

My father loved animals. We had cats too, for the mice.

Arsenio finished drinking, and my father took away the bowl. You look tired, he said to me. There's a raccoon's mask around your eyes.

I am tired, I said.

I'm glad to see you working hard, he said. He covered Arsenio with a red plaid blanket and left the kitchen. I listened to his footsteps going to his room. I went back to my book.

So I grew up, I was smart. When I was four years old, I knew how to read and write in Spanish. When I was ten, I could read anything from the Tico newspaper. When I was fourteen, I graduated with the highest mark in my school. I knew how to work.

Ricky doesn't know anything. Fourteen, and last year he was in the sixth grade. This year again he'd be in the sixth. He failed all his subjects. The teacher on the report card said she can't believe Ricky tried to learn.

I don't understand, I said to him. You're not a stupid boy. Why do you do this to yourself?

It's the language, he said. I have problems with this language.

But that was lies, lies. They have special classes. He learned English better than me. To talk to his friends he knew English very fine. And to me. I said something in Spanish, he answered in English. He knew I didn't like it. I don't love English. I speak it because I have to speak it, but at home in my own house I like to keep my own language. He knew how to curse in English, no problem.

Sometimes he didn't go to school at all. In the winter once a week they called me. Where is your son? I didn't know where he was. Did they think I just sat at home all the time and watched what Ricky was doing? All day I worked. Some days I left the house six or six-thirty. I took a bus to where the women live on the other side of the city, where the nice houses are. I didn't mind waking up early. That's how it was for me all my life. If I had two houses that day, I liked to start early.

I tried to bribe him. I said Ricky, if you go to school, I'll buy you something. I'll buy you one of those big TVs.

I have some money. I get forty dollars for every house. They pay me cash. What I get I put away. I have always been very careful with my money.

I don't want a TV, he said.

What do you want? I said.

I want to go back to Costa Rica.

Why? I said. What did you have over there that you don't have here?

I hate it here, he said.

All summer I worried what would happen when school started again. When I rode on the bus past the school and I saw the sign Welcome Class of '00, I felt my stomach turn like a fish. In this country I don't know what they do to you if your son won't go to school. I was afraid to go to jail.

●　●　●

One day not so long ago I was thinking about Arsenio. We need a dog, I told Eddie. Shyla would like a dog.

There was a house I cleaned where she had a small curly white dog. When I tried to vacuum the rug, the dog jumped at the vacuum. So then I put it in the bedroom. I said okay, doggie, you stay here. He barked and barked and scraped at the door. But before she came home I let him out.

I don't like the little dogs. They remind me of rodents, rats or *guatusa* like you see in my country. There they don't have all these different kinds of dogs like people have over here. They're all one dog. Big and skinny, with short brown fur. I told Eddie I want a big one.

A dog is a lot of work, he said.

Growing up, we always had a dog.

You have a son you can't do something with, he said. How are you going to have a dog?

Don't talk to me like that, I said.

I'm just saying how it is. You can't keep a big dog in an apartment.

First I was angry at him for it. But then I started to think maybe he's right. A dog is like a baby that doesn't grow up. My father used to say having Arsenio was like having a fifth child.

I'm not having any more children. I'm going to have an operation for it. Jackie said don't do that, what if you change your mind, but I told her I'm not going to change. There's a clinic I heard about where you can go. It's not too expensive. You go in and you can leave the same day. I know what I'm saying. Some things I change my mind, but not about that. I had enough with children.

5

I t started from the first day he came here, back in
October.

He got off the plane with one black bag. When I
looked at him, I thought he looks very different. If I saw him
someplace, I would never know it was him. He got very tall,
and he had his hair cut short in the back so you could see the
white skin through it. He had some dark hair on his top lip.
Not a lot, but it was there. I couldn't believe this was him.
This boy was my son. We stood looking at each other.

I didn't want to come, he said.

What do you say to this? I didn't want you to come also?
Why did you do this to your hair? I said.

We took a taxi to the apartment. In the car I kept turning
to look at him and then look away so he wouldn't notice. I saw
he wasn't really so different. It was the same face. The more I
looked at him, the more I saw he hadn't changed. His eyes, his
mouth. Under the hair, the mark on his lip was still there.

How's your grandma? I asked him.

He shrugged.

I didn't say anything more. I had to pay attention to the cab. You have to be careful when you take a taxi that they don't bring you another way. If they think you don't know the place, they do that. Once it was cold and I didn't want to wait for a bus, so I took a taxi home from work. He drove me all the way down to the end of the street and then came back again on the opposite side. When I saw what he's doing I thought I'll get out of the cab at a red light. I won't pay for this ride. He can't do anything to me, I thought. He doesn't know my name or where I live. But I didn't do it. I was afraid he would start shouting and the police would come.

Now I'm always careful to watch how we go. When I get in the cab, I say right away take me this way and this way. I look out the window for the things I know.

Ricky sat looking out the other window. It was raining. Everything was gray. The sky and the sidewalks and the buildings. We drove past a lot of buildings with their windows broken. In some other ones you could see women working at sewing machines at long tables.

This is it, I said.

The taxi turned onto my street. We went by the drugstore, the laundromat, the Thai restaurant with the plates of dusty plastic food in the window. There was one man sitting by himself. He had his coat on the chair across from him, like he was pretending there was another person there. Lonely, I thought. I had never seen him before. Then we came to my building. It's a brick building on the corner with four floors. There are other brick buildings around it. They all look the same. But the one on the corner is nicer because it has some grass. There's a swing there and two animals for the children to play on. Shyla likes to sit on the duck. It's broken, but she doesn't know. Sometimes there's other children.

There are a lot of Hispanic people living in these buildings. I prefer to live with Hispanic people because I understand them. I know what they do that I like, what they do that I don't like. When you want to be comfortable, it's good to get a place with people like you. Shyla has a little boyfriend here.

Upstairs, it's not a very big apartment. There's the bedroom where I sleep with Shyla, and the main room with the table and the TV and the couch that folds out. The kitchen is along one wall. It's not a real kitchen, just a sink and a stove and a small refrigerator all crowded together, with a little piece of a counter and a strip of linoleum on the floor. Eddie blocked off one corner of the main room with some shelves he made from wood. It was supposed to be for the baby, but after my mother called to say Ricky is coming I told him my son will have to sleep there. He wasn't happy about it. There's no other choice, I said. He's not sleeping out here. I put a cot behind the shelves. There's no door, so I hung a curtain.

Then the day before he came I looked at the room and saw it was very empty. It looked like a jail room, no window even. So I went out and bought a poster of a lighthouse on some rocks and put it up on the wall over the cot. It was a very nice lighthouse, white with a red roof and yellow light making a yellow path on the water.

Here's where you'll sleep, I told Ricky, and I waited to see if he would like it. But he didn't say anything. He put his bag on the cot and started taking out his things.

Well, I'll leave you alone, I said.

That night when Eddie came to the apartment, I called Ricky to come out of his room.

This is Ricky, I said.

Eddie looked at him. He looked at Eddie. I knew right away they didn't like each other.

You live here? Ricky said.

I live downstairs, Eddie said. But you'll see me around.

Ricky's face was empty. You couldn't see anything there.

I hope you don't give your mama any trouble, Eddie said, putting his hands on my shoulders.

Ricky leaned against the shelves. Is there food? he said.

I don't know, I said.

I'll make us some supper, Eddie said. No problem.

Eddie likes to cook. Those are his hobbies, making things with wood and cooking. He takes pictures of the things he cooks and keeps them in a scrapbook, so if he wants to make it again he can do that. Sometimes he cooks American food, hamburgers or something like that, but I never eat it. I don't like meat. When I was a little girl in my father's house, I ate meat because I had to eat it, but not anymore. Not since I came to this country. Maybe a small piece of chicken but that is all.

Why won't you eat it? Eddie asked me. I'm a good cook.

I'm not hungry, I said. I don't eat a lot.

I was always very careful what I eat. If I made a chicken, I washed it very carefully, first in cold water, then hot water, then again cold. Then I soaked it in salt water for one hour. I took off all the skin. Then I cooked it. I only eat what I cook myself. Beans and rice, some vegetables, a fruit. In Costa Rica you cook red beans, and you pour the red water in the rice so the rice is red. We cooked corn and potatoes, beans and sweet potatoes. Maybe that's why I'm so thin, because I don't like to eat meat. My brothers are all big men. And my father was.

I see you're not much of an eater, the doctor said when I was pregnant with Shyla. You have to eat.

So I told him I'll die if I eat meat.

It's not in my stomach. It's in my head. I know that. My mother never ate any food that was red. Because when she was growing up her grandfather used to take her into the rain forest and he taught her don't eat anything red. Red is poisonous. She could never get rid of that. Even the small red land crabs she wouldn't eat. Other people love to eat those crabs. They're like a treat.

It was in her head. So I am also that way. There are things you take from your parents.

Eddie keeps an aloe plant on the counter in the kitchen. It has long arms that reach like green snakes along the counter to the sink. It's not a pretty plant, but it's good for burns. You cut a piece of the leaf and put the juice on your skin. He says it works better than any kind of medicine. If I came to the kitchen and I saw the plant was smaller, I knew he was cooking again and he burned himself.

The night Ricky came Eddie cooked meat and yellow rice. For myself, I took a little cereal. There's only two chairs by the table, so I sat on the couch. We turned on the TV and watched it while we ate. Ricky ate maybe a pound of rice.

It's good, no? Eddie said. I make good rice.

It's just rice, Ricky said. It's not different from my grandma's rice.

That's impossible, Eddie said. It's my own recipe.

Ricky shrugged. Food's food, he said.

Eddie's eyes were thin, like pencils. That's what you say, he said. I make good rice.

He stood up from the table. Ricky stayed sitting. Under the voices from the TV, I felt their silence in the air like electricity.

Eddie turned to me. Cereal is not a supper, he said. Take something else.

I don't want something else.

Fine, he said. Do what you want, then. He took the plates off the table and scraped the extra rice into the garbage. The fork made a sharp angry sound against the plates.

Why are you wasting it? I said.

Are you going to eat it?

I didn't answer.

Ricky was watching the TV. He didn't say anything, but you knew he was there. And after that, he was always there. Even when he was not in the apartment he was there, taking my air, filling my space, all these months, until I think I will go crazy.

C H A P T E R

6

C lass is supposed to end at seven o'clock. Most weeks she keeps us late. Don't any of you plan on catching the seven o'clock movie, she said the first day. But tonight I ran out of there very fast. Someone said where are you rushing to, and I said I have to pick up my baby at the neighbor. That's not true, she doesn't care if I come a few minutes late. She has her own baby Shyla's age, and she says what's the difference one more. But they don't know that at the school. I'm not going to stay and talk about what did you get on the stupid test.

The Adult Education Center is a small brick building with one room. There's a circle of wooden desks with wooden chairs attached. I always hated the desks. All day I clean houses and wash floors and nothing hurts me, but after fifteen minutes sitting in those chairs I have a backache. It's not from me. I know how to sit. My father always said sit up straight, stand up straight. Every night he made me stand against the wall, and he put his hand between my back and the wall. He measured the distance there with his fingers. There shouldn't be any empty space, he said. So I pressed my back against the wall to stand up straighter. Some children grow up and their spine is crooked, but not Gloria. I'll never be like the old ladies you see on the bus, bent over like trees after a rain storm.

The class is three hours. I keep moving around in my seat, trying to get comfortable. I look at the men with legs bigger than my waist, and I think to myself how can they sit so still?

There's twelve people in the class. They're from different places, Guatemala, Ethiopia, Haiti. I am the only Tico.

For me it's hard to go there after work. I have to leave Shyla extra time at the neighbor. I pay her for it. Shyla doesn't like it when I leave her there. She cries by the door. The neighbor says she won't eat. If she gives her food, Shyla keeps it in her mouth until her cheeks puff out and then she spits it out. She wants only me to feed her. When I bring her home at night, sometimes she drinks nine bottles of milk. Her cheeks are fat with milk. But I have to leave her. Eddie won't take her.

English is a hard language for me. When I came to this country, I listened very carefully. I paid a lot of attention to hear how they say this, how they say that. So I learned to talk and to understand. In my job this is very important. Because she says you have to clean this or do this and if you don't do it she'll be angry. Sometimes she leaves a note. I try to read what it says there. If you can't read it you can get into trouble. Once when I first started working, the note said don't wash the purple dress hanging in the laundry room, and I washed it and it shrank from a dress to a shirt. When I saw what happened, I cried and cried. I thought she'll fire me and tell all her friends. And I need to work to make money to send to my mother in Costa Rica. She didn't fire me. But that was one of the reasons why I said I want to come to this school.

I took different classes. Sometimes I took one, sometimes I didn't. It's a lot of work. But when Ricky came here in the fall I started to take again. And this summer I said I will take. That's how it is. You start to think how to get away from the apartment.

At the beginning of class she says to mingle. That means you're supposed to walk around the room and say things to the other people in English. The first weeks we always said the same things, because we didn't know each other and we were embarrassed to make a mistake.

Hi.

Hi.

How are you?

Good. How are you?

I have a backache. I have to stand.

But then later we started talking about different things.

Do you have family here?

I have my husband and two daughters. You have a husband?

I have a baby. I have a son came here from Costa Rica.

Very good.

No. It's no good.

Why?

He plays Nintendo.

All the boys play Nintendo.

There are other things.

What things?

I'd start to say something more. But then the time for talking was over, and there was the real class.

I always sit in the front of the room. I have a little blue notebook and I write down everything she puts on the blackboard and everything she says. If I miss something, I say can you please say that again. She said you don't have to write down every word, Gloria, but that is the way I do it. Then when I come home at night, I copy it again. So I will learn how to write good English. Because sometimes when I'm cleaning I need the woman to buy certain things, and if she's not home I have to write a note. I'm very careful what I use to clean. I only use the things I know, and if I don't have them I can't clean the house. I used to write down how the word sounds, but sometimes she didn't understand and she didn't buy it. Then the house isn't so clean.

Every two weeks there is a test. I stay up late at night to study, like I used to do in Costa Rica. I never failed a test.

But tonight I came late. The bus was late. I had to take two buses from the house, and I waited and waited for that second bus. When I came in, she said you're late, sit down, here is your test. I was hot and out of breath from running. I took some pencils from my bag and lined them up on my desk. I like to have a lot of pencils in case they break. I'm always afraid my pencil will break and I'll fail the test.

I opened the test to the first page. I saw I didn't know anything. You were supposed to read the story and answer some questions, but when I tried to read it, it didn't make sense. It was a story about a boy learning to drive a car. There were a lot of words I didn't understand.

I thought I'd skip it and come back to it later. So I turned to another part. But that part also I didn't know. I started to feel my heart beating. I looked around the room. It was very quiet. Other people were taking the test.

When I was young and went to school, I used to get sick every time there was a test. I got a stomachache and sometimes I threw up. Nobody knew about it. I'd go out to the yard behind the school and throw up and then come back inside and take the test. My heart would beat in my chest like a bird hitting a window, so I thought for sure everyone could hear it.

But that was a long time ago. I said to myself, Gloria, you work hard. You know how to take a test. I found one question that I knew. Then I found another one. I started to write.

I had maybe ten minutes to take that test. It felt like only ten minutes. The room was very hot. My hair was coming out of my ponytail and sticking to my neck. There was a fan in the front, but it just blew the hot air across the desks. Someone tied some pieces of toilet paper to it, and the white paper moving made it hard for me to pay attention to the test. Even when I looked down at my desk, I could see them waving in the corner of my eye, like streamers at a party. The fan kept blowing my pencils on the floor. I had to stop writing to pick them up.

Time, she said.

One little minute, I said.

I wanted to check if I did all the questions. I was the last person to hand it in.

She marked the papers right away. She circled them with green pen. I stood by her desk and counted how many right, how many wrong. I couldn't believe it. I thought I must have counted wrong.

I'm sorry, she said. You'll have to take it again. She gave me three books to read, and she said when you're ready come back to me.

I just kept staring at the paper. How could it happen? The last test I got an eighty-four. It wasn't the highest mark, but it wasn't the lowest mark either. It was better than eighty. I never got under eighty.

Gloria? she said. Are you all right?

You don't understand, I said.

It's only one test. You'll make it up. You nearly passed.

She touched my hand.

I can't fail, I screamed. But the scream stayed inside my head. She smiled at me and turned her head to talk to another student. I grabbed the books and ran out of the room.

I sat on the bus. My hands were shaking. It wasn't a fair test. I don't know anything about driving. I never drove a car. The only thing I ever drove was a horse.

A man with a bag sat down next to me. He said something, but I didn't understand what he said. I thought maybe he wants to do something to me. What does he have in that bag? I got off the bus even though it wasn't my stop and walked the rest of the way home. When I stopped to pick up Shyla the neighbor said something to me, and I said something back but I don't know what.

My father's voice was ringing in my head.

● ● ●

Since Carlos called to say Ricky ran away, I couldn't stop thinking about him. Where he is, what he's doing. Yesterday he called me from a pay phone someplace in California. He had nothing. No food, no money, nothing.

What are you doing? I said.

Sitting on a bench.

Where were you going?

I don't know. Nowhere.

I told him I would send money, and this morning I sent it.

You take this money and go back to Carlos, I said. You hear me?

I hear.

All day I was thinking did he get back there yet. Maybe that's why I failed the test, because I wasn't concentrating. I thought when I get home I will call Carlos to see if he's there.

But now Ricky is just a shadow in the corner of my mind. My father's voice is everything. It's very big, it fills my head like a balloon. You disappoint me, Gloria. I'm not raising children to be idiots.

Then I come to my apartment. I breathe in the smells and feel the heat on my face and hear other voices from the people I know going on with their lives. They push away my father's voice, and there's room in my head for other things. For Ricky. And I know right away there's trouble.

There's a saying in Spanish, Move on like a big elephant. My father used to say that. You do what you have to do. Your son comes to this country and gives you trouble, you still get up in the morning and go to work. Clean the house. Go to school at night. Come home and wash up and study and get ready for the next day.

Soon after Ricky came to me, I took him to the public school and signed him up there. They gave him a test to see what class to put him. I had to fill out some forms. While Ricky was taking his test, a woman sat behind a desk and asked me questions.

The office was small and hot. It smelled like ink and coffee and a cleaner I didn't recognize. I tried to think what kind it could be, but I didn't know. Maybe they use it only for schools. Outside in the hall I could hear doors slamming and kids talking. I heard some Spanish there.

In my country you had to wear a uniform to school. If you're rich, if you're poor, you still had to wear it. The girls had a gray skirt with pleats and the boys had pants and a blue tie. But here I see in the halls they wear different things. Jeans, T-shirts, whatever they want to wear, they can do that. Maybe that's why they don't learn so good over here, because they don't have a uniform. There's a sign hanging that you have to wear shoes. Who would think to come to school without shoes?

The woman tapped her nails on the desk. She had black skin and short yellow hair tight against her head, like a shower hat. I thought the hair was too yellow and too short. It made her look like a man. Her voice also was like a man's.

Are you a single parent? she said, looking at the forms.

Yes, I said. I was very careful to talk English in that school. I wanted them to know I can speak this language.

Is there another number we can contact in case of emergency?

This number.

But someone else. A friend, a relative?

I saw her looking at my pregnant stomach. I thought should I put Eddie's number there? But I didn't want them calling Eddie. He wouldn't like it, he wouldn't know what to do about it. No, I said. It's only me.

She was thinking I couldn't handle it alone, I wasn't strong enough for it. But I told her I am his mother. If you have something, you call me.

So that's why all winter they were calling. When the phone rang at night, loud and long like a screaming voice, I knew who it was. Sometimes I didn't answer it. If I had a hard day at work, I didn't want to talk to her. I come home, take a shower, rub some medicine cream into my body where the muscles hurt. Take another shower. I don't have to talk to people I don't want in my own apartment.

Even though I was pregnant, I still went to work. The women said take some time off, and Eddie said I have money, but I wanted to work. I'm not that kind to sit at home and take money from a man. Other women maybe, but not Gloria. That's not how I was raised.

Well, some light dusting, then, she said. No floors. If I catch you doing the floors, I'm going to send you home.

I take a lot of time to do the floors. In Costa Rica we have wood floors and we clean them every day. On Monday you wax it. The next day you polish it. In some places they use a coconut. The outside is like sandpaper. If you cut it open and attach one half on the end of a wooden stick, it becomes a brush.

It's like a ritual. Your house has to be clean all over. Under the couch, under the bed. It's how we grow up and how we live.

When I came to this country, they said Gloria, you don't have to put so much energy into the floors, but I did it this way because this is the way I know. First I swept to get rid of all the big things. Then I washed it and let it dry ten or fifteen minutes. Then I polished it. It's harder maybe, but it's better. I was never afraid of what is hard.

I hated to do less. How can I leave there if the floors are still dirty? It looks like I don't know how to clean a house. Once in my father's house I forgot to polish the floor and there were guests. After they left, he took me outside, behind the big rock. It's a disgrace, he said. I'm ashamed to have you for my daughter. I knew he was right. So when I was pregnant and couldn't do the floors in the houses where I worked, to make up for it I did other things. I ironed the underwear, or I fixed things.

I went around the houses, looking for what was broken. One woman had a dryer that when you turned it on the door fell open. I thought I can do something about that. I got a metal hanger from the bedroom and twisted it into a hook. I attached it to the door handle. Then with a string I connected the hook to the top part of the dryer. I think she was a little bit surprised when she saw it. That's some contraption you rigged up in the laundry room, she said. I didn't understand what she meant, but I thought maybe she's worried now the dryer won't work right. So I showed her it worked fine.

At another house I saw the kitchen table had one leg shorter than the other one. I cut a piece of cardboard to go under it so it would stand straight. It was like a new table again.

The only thing I couldn't fix was the vacuum cleaner in the green house with the shutters. The woman, Brenda, had an old vacuum that didn't pick up anything. After you vacuumed, there were still balls of dust and pieces of dirt on the floor. And the house is very big, with many corners for the dust to live. So I tried to fix it. I took it apart and put it back together again. It's a big heavy machine with lots of parts. When I was finished, I had an extra part, a plastic tube. I had no idea where this came from. I didn't know what to do with it.

I was standing there holding the piece in my hand, and I heard Brenda coming down the hall. Very fast, I opened the closet and threw it in. I turned on the vacuum. It was worse than before. Now it made a noise like a broken jeep. It still didn't pick up the dirt.

You need to get a new vacuum, I shouted on top of the noise.

What? she shouted back.

I turned it off. I said you need a new one.

Yes, I know. It's on my list.

She made a face. That one sounds awful, doesn't it? I didn't realize it was so bad.

I didn't say anything.

I thought for sure she'll have a new vacuum cleaner the next time I come. But when I opened the closet it was the same old vacuum, with the gray hose curled around it like a sleeping animal. The noise gave me a headache. After I vacuumed, I went around the room, picking up the rest of the dirt with my hands. I didn't like it. I always felt there's more dirt, hiding in the dark places deep inside the carpet. But I thought she was a nice woman, so I did it for her.

One night I dreamed she got a new one. It was red, very small and light. You didn't have to do anything. It moved around the room almost by itself, and your feet didn't have to touch the floor. But it was just a dream. The last time I was there, a few weeks ago, she still had the one with the hose. Then I stopped working for her. She got someone else, and she didn't even wait until I came to the house to tell me. She called on the phone. It turns out she wasn't so nice like I thought.

I was always a good worker. I worked until the last minute before the bus. One day in one of the houses I finished my regular things a little bit early, and I was looking for something to do. I decided I will arrange the drawer in her bed table. Because once when I opened it a hundred things came spilling out. Scarves, lipsticks, birthday cards, candles, pictures in frames, pictures not in frames. I never saw somebody with so many things. There were stockings with holes and earrings with no match. If I can fix up that drawer that will be good, I thought.

I got a box to put the earrings in and went into the bedroom. It was very neat. The mirror was clean, the painting was straight, the cover on the bed was the same all the way around. The room smelled like the lemon I use to polish the wood. I smiled. That's what I like about it. You can always know when Gloria was here.

I stood by the bed. It's a very pretty bed. The cover has little pink and yellow and purple flowers, and there's tall pink pillows that I made taller with my hands. All of a sudden I wanted to sit down there. Usually when I'm cleaning I never sit on the bed. It's not my place. But now I sat. The mattress is very soft. I bounced a little bit up and down. I wondered what it feels like to sleep in that bed.

There was no one at home. The house was very quiet. Very carefully, I lay down on the pillows.

I closed my eyes. I was lying in a field of flowers. Over my head was a bright blue sky. I didn't recognize the place, but I knew it was back in Costa Rica. The wind was rocking the grass. My dress fell up over my bare knees, and the grass tickled the backs of my legs. I heard birds singing. Everything was very far away.

Then I heard my father's voice, calling me. Gloria! I jumped up. I was dizzy. The field was spinning around me in colored stripes. I'm coming! I was breathing hard. I couldn't remember where I was.

The grass turned into the rug. I was back in the bedroom. I could feel my heartbeat, in my chest and in my throat.

I tiptoed out of the room, like a robber who is afraid to be discovered. In the hall I stopped. The house was so quiet. The only sound was the big clock at the bottom of the stairs. The pendulum swung back and forth like a gold sun. The noise made the quiet longer and deeper.

I don't know why, but I turned from the hall into the little girl's room. I wasn't thinking about it. My feet just moved there. She has a small bed with a yellow cover. I lay down also on this one. If you sleep in someone else's bed do you have their dreams? I thought. I tried to think what a little girl dreams. She's a nice girl. Maybe she dreams about growing up and getting married and having a baby. She has baby dolls with pretty lace dresses all along her shelves. I touched my hand to my round stomach. What did I dream when I was that age? I didn't remember. I remember I had a rag doll with black yarn hair that my mother made for me. It was so old it had no face. Its skin was gray.

I tried hard, but I couldn't remember even one thing I dreamed. I got up quickly and left that room.

There was one more bedroom upstairs. The boy's room. Everything in this room is baseball. Baseball lamp, baseball posters, baseball bed. The blankets are blue and white stripes. Even though I just washed them, they smelled like the boy. It must be from the soap he uses. I pressed my cheek on the pillow.

He's thirteen, the same age as Ricky. But he looks much

younger. He's very skinny and his face is white and smooth. There's no hair there at all. His mother calls him J.J. He calls her Mommy. Ricky doesn't call me anything.

I started to think what does Ricky smell like? Maybe he also smells like soap if you come close to him. I used to know how my children smell. If one of the boys was sick, if he had a fever, I knew right away by how he smelled. I didn't have to touch him even.

Maybe Ricky would like a baseball poster, I thought, instead of the lighthouse. When I get home, I'll remember to ask him. I wonder where you buy such a poster. If you have to go to a game for it. In this country, boys go to baseball games together with their father. They eat hot dogs.

I almost fell asleep lying there. I felt my mind moving out of the room. I was again in the field with flowers, but this time Ricky and Miguel were with me. We were playing baseball. Ricky hit the ball and I reached for it but it was too high, too fast, over my head. I started to run after it. But then my father was calling me again. Gloria! Don't make me have to come and find you! The ball fell somewhere and was lost in the grass.

It was getting late. I had to hurry if I didn't want to miss my bus. I took my money where she left it on the kitchen counter behind the spice rack and my shoes from behind the door. I felt bad about the drawer. Next week, I thought.

When I came home, I was very tired. Eddie was chopping onions and green peppers into little squares. Ricky wasn't home.

Do you want some supper? Eddie said.

No, I said. I'm exhausted.

Gloria, you need to eat. You heard the doctor. A baby is like a parasite. He takes everything.

His eyes were red and wet in the corners from the onions. I'm fine, I said. I eat.

I went to bed before ten o'clock.

But in my own bed I couldn't sleep. I lay there staring into the dark. I don't know how long it was, and then Eddie crawled in next to me. He touched me. His fingers smelled like onions. Your shoulders are so stiff, he whispered. Relax.

I couldn't relax. It was like I was waiting for something, but I didn't know what. Only later, when I heard the key in the door and Ricky go to his room, did I feel my body get softer.

Just before I fell asleep I remembered about the poster. I thought maybe I'll get up, but Eddie's hand was on my stomach, covering the baby. I'll ask him in the morning, I thought.

But I never did. In the morning I went to work before he woke up. When I came back, Eddie was there, and Ricky stayed all night in front of the TV. The next day was the same. There was never a good time for it. Then one day I walked past and the curtain was open and I saw he put his own poster there. A red sports car.

●　●　●

I stopped working for two weeks when Shyla was born. They wanted me to take longer, but I couldn't do it. I sat in the house all day with the baby until I thought I will go crazy. Jackie brought me a bulb in a pot, an amaryllis. I waited every day to see if it would grow. The first thing in the

morning, before I had my coffee even, I went to the pot on
the windowsill to check if something had come up yet. The
last thing at night before I went to sleep I poured water from
a mug into the pot.

Ricky came in and out. He did what he did. I didn't tell
him anything. I was too tired for it. He looked very big, not
like a normal boy. I would hold Shyla with her tiny fingers
and toes, and then when I saw Ricky I thought Santa María,
he looks like a monster. His fingers are like sausages. His feet
can crush me to pieces. Even the pores of his skin looked too
big. I was afraid of him. That's silly, I thought. After you
have a baby, you don't think right.

When Shyla took a nap, I lay on the bed and watched the
shape of the sun on the rug. I decided I hate that rug in the
bedroom. It's an ugly color, not white, not brown. What kind
of person would pick a rug like that? I wanted to change it. I
kept thinking to ask Eddie about it. There's something I
wanted to ask you, I'd say when he came. What's that? he'd
say. But then I'd forget what it was.

I stood by the window and poked the dirt in the pot. I
didn't see anything there. Even though I was still tired, I was
glad to go back to work.

Eddie worries. That's the kind of man he is. He worries about the neighborhood, that it isn't safe. He doesn't like for me to go out at night. Sometimes I have to go out, I have to do laundry. If I have something small to wash, like Shyla's undershirts, I bring it with me to work and I do them over there when I do the laundry. But if there's too much I do it at night when I come home. The laundromat is on the next block, by the Thai restaurant.

I don't like it, Eddie says. It's not safe.

Don't be silly, I say. There's people living all around. Someone would hear something. They'd open a window.

This isn't Costa Rica, he says. You could be murdered on the street and nobody would even look outside. They have their own troubles, they don't want to get involved. Last year a woman was raped in an alley at one o'clock in the afternoon and nobody did anything. When the police asked about it, they said they had no idea anything was happening.

I said if you don't want me going out, you do the laundry. But he won't do that. He says washing clothes is the woman's job.

He gave me a present. A can of pepper spray. It's a little can, you're supposed to put it on the ring with your keys. At least if you're going out, take this with you, he said. But I never did. I don't need this, I thought. I put it someplace in a drawer.

One night I was coming home with my laundry in the cart, and someone reached out and grabbed me. A hand covered my mouth. I couldn't scream. I couldn't breathe. I thought I'm going to die.

I tried to fight, to bite his hand. I can't die. If I die what will happen to my baby?

Then I saw it was Eddie.

I wanted to kill him.

Pig, I screamed. What the hell are you doing?

Did you see anyone running to save you? he said. Did you see any open windows?

You are a pig, I said. I hate you.

I didn't talk to him for a week. When he called I hung up. When he came upstairs I didn't answer the door.

I did it for you, he said through the door. You know I did it for you.

He left flowers in the hall, red and white.

• • •

I was with Eddie from the first day I moved to the apartment. I met him even before I moved here. He got me the place. Then that first day, when I was unpacking my things, I saw the wall was breaking under the window and I called him to fix it. He came to look. It's a wasps' nest, he said right away. Listen.

I put my ear near the wall and I could hear them inside there.

I'll take care of it for you, he said. No problem. He came back in one quick minute with a paper bag and black rubber gloves. He cut two holes in the bag for his eyes and put it over his head. He put on the gloves. Stay back, he said.

The wall was like tissue. He reached both hands in there and pulled out the nest. Big black wasps buzzed around his head. I gave a little scream.

He pulled me outside to the hall and slammed the door. When he took off the bag, his hair stuck up all over his head. He looked like a little boy who just woke up. I started to laugh.

Hey, what's so funny? he said. But he was laughing also. I thought I like this man. I like someone who makes me laugh.

Did you ever get stung? I asked him.

Never.

He took me downstairs to his apartment until they could come spray. I'll cook you supper, he said, and he showed me pictures of his different foods in the scrapbook. Pick something. Whatever you want. He turned through the pages. Rice with meat, rice with vegetables, some kinds of spaghetti with fancy sauces. See, I even do Italian. Do you like Italian?

I saw his hands were not too clean. I said no, thank you, but the pictures look very nice.

I take good pictures, he said.

He poured some Coca-Cola. At least have a drink, he said.

We sat in an orange beanbag chair, and he told me about where he grew up, in a little fishing village in Puerto Rico. He lived in a house of one room with his parents and his brother and sister and two grandmothers. There were nets and hooks covering the ground in front of the house. His father was away a lot on the boat. It was Eddie's job to take care of the nets.

I wanted something better than my father had, he said. I wanted real shoes. I wanted a car.

Because they used to go without shoes, even outside, and once he stepped on a hook. It went up into his foot and he got an infection there. The bone turned soft and green.

A doctor probably would have cut it off, Eddie said, but we didn't have a doctor. I'm lucky I can walk.

He still limps from it.

They were good people, he said. Poorer than rats, but everyone was a friend. If you came to that village, they wouldn't let you leave without a hot meal. That's how I learned to cook, from watching my grandmothers.

The time passed. I listened. Eddie's story is very different from mine. My father always bought us good shoes. Once a year, before school started, we went to a store in town and a man with a mustache measured our feet for it. Then my father picked them out. He knew what were the best shoes. Sometimes I wanted shoes with a shiny silver buckle, but he said no, those aren't good, you have to get these. Because the buckle can break or something like that. When you're a child you don't think of these things. We left the old shoes in the store for the poor kids and wore the new ones to go home.

I took care of those shoes. I tried to keep them nice. I remember once I was playing on the beach, not paying attention, and when I looked up my shoes were floating out in the waves. I almost drowned to get them back. A wave knocked me down, I tried to stand up, I breathed water and salt into my lungs.

But I didn't tell Eddie anything about this. I didn't talk about my own family. I never talked too much to people about my life before I came here.

The windows turned black with night. Stay here tonight, Eddie said. There'll be a smell from the spray. He gave me a T-shirt to sleep in. It was too big, down to my knees, and the neck fell down around my shoulders. Eddie's body was soft and warm, with little folds in his stomach. I squeezed his skin between my fingers. It was a long time since I was with a man. After that, we were together.

Later he painted the apartment for me. The people who lived here before wrote things on the walls. There were words in pencil in all the rooms, even the bathroom. In the kitchen over the stove it said Eat Death in red marker. If you look close you can still see it through the white paint. Eddie said it's probably a curse in English.

When I got pregnant I wasn't so sure about it, because the world isn't easy and who needs another baby. But Eddie was breaking with happiness. To whoever would listen he talked about the baby. Then after she was born he was even more. He loves this baby. All the time he wanted to take me shopping, buy something for the baby. Shyla needs this, Shyla needs that. I told him she will be spoiled, but he just laughed and bought another something. Clothes and toys and little animals. The money didn't matter. Only the best things for the baby.

When I was a kid, he said, my mother used to recycle the Christmas presents. I had a bicycle. I'd ride it all year round. Then in November, December, it would suddenly disappear. I wouldn't have it for a while. And then on Christmas it would be back again. Only now it was a different color. Blue, instead of red. It was the same thing with my sister. She had a baby doll. Every Christmas she'd get it back with a different outfit.

He touched the baby's cheek. Shyla will have a dozen baby dolls, he said.

But if she cried, she was my baby. He wouldn't change the diaper even. If she got sick I'd have to call the woman and say my baby's sick, I can't work today. Because the neighbor wouldn't watch her if she was sick. She didn't want her own baby to catch something.

Some women didn't make it easy for me. How sick? she'd say.

Sick. She's throwing up.

Can't you get a sitter? I really need you here.

So I'd try to get someone. Jackie's older daughter, Michaela, who's twelve, sometimes came. If there was a vacation from school or something like that. But I didn't like to ask her. What does a girl twelve years old know about taking care of a baby? Maybe she'll drop her. Maybe worse. There's stories I see on TV. But Eddie didn't want anything to do with it. If I called him he was downstairs, working on the toy box. I'm busy, he said. I'll pay for the baby-sitter.

For him the baby is like the laundry. It's the woman's job.

•   •   •

You can't be angry forever. Eddie isn't perfect, but he's comfortable. He's the only man I ever had. If he didn't come upstairs, some days I would talk to no one.

I opened the door and took in the flowers. In ten minutes he called me on the phone. Pour a can of Sprite into the water, he said. It will make them live longer.

I said I will try to remember to carry the pepper spray in my pocket.

There's something else you should have, Eddie said. Just to keep in the apartment.

He said it's very important, living here, for everyone to have a gun.

Let me tell you a story, he said. Once I was driving my truck and I got too close to the car in front of me. And the man stopped and pulled out a gun. I thought that was it. It's all over. But lucky for me, there was a cop around the corner. Nothing happened. I went out right away and bought a gun.

I told him I don't need a gun because I don't drive. Once he tried to teach me, but I said no, I'm too nervous for it. Because my father used to tell me that when I wanted to drive his jeep, and he was right. Eddie said there's nothing to be nervous about, look at all the idiots who are out on the road. But when I got in the truck my hands were shaking. The front wheel twisted. You see? I said. I stopped the truck and got out. If you want to get home, you drive. After that, I never even got into the driver's seat.

Eddie said anyway you need a gun. People can come into your house and take everything you have, maybe take your money. If you don't have a gun, you can't do anything.

He put it in my hands. It was small, but it was very heavy.

I can't shoot this, I said.

We used to have guns on the farm. Everyone had, to protect against wild animals. My father had five guns. My brothers went out hunting with them, but I wasn't allowed to touch them, even to clean. You're too nervous, my father said, like he said about the jeep. They hung on the wall, big to small, and once a month he took them down to clean them himself. He sat on the steps and polished them with a yellow wax until they shone. I watched his hands. He had strong fingers, hard palms. His thumbs could bend all the way back. I stood on the step and if he was in a good mood he would show me.

Anyone can shoot a gun, Eddie said. You just point it where you want it to go and pull the trigger.

I couldn't do it, I said.

If you had to you would, he said.

He said put it someplace safe. In his own apartment he kept a gun in the refrigerator. In the drawer where other people put the lettuce. It's the safest place, he said. But I won't have a gun in there with the food. I put it under my bed. I won't ever use it, I thought. I was careful to put it far back, where Shyla can't reach. She's not strong enough to do something with it, but it's good to be careful. There are stories about what happens when children play with a gun.

I didn't tell anyone about it. It's not their business what I keep in my apartment.

When Ricky came, Eddie changed his mind. Maybe I'll keep the gun for you, he said one day. I'd prefer to keep it.

But I said no. You gave it to me, it's my gun now.

Because I was used to having it, even though I knew I

wouldn't use it. I don't like it when they give something and then take it away.

I knew what Eddie was thinking.

I'm telling you, he's not dangerous like that, I said. He doesn't even know it's there. He never goes in my bedroom.

Well, it's good protection for you, Eddie said. But make sure he doesn't find it.

He gave me a leather case to keep it in. You wouldn't know there was a gun in there.

• • •

He used to warn me all the time about Ricky. You have to do something. You're his mother. But I didn't know what to do. Some things I know. I know how to get a job. I know how to work. But how to be his mother I didn't know.

I was washing his clothes, and I found a cigarette in his pocket. I hate it when people smoke. There was one house I cleaned where the husband smoked, and when I came home everything smelled from it. My hair, my clothes, everything. There's different kinds of smoke. The smoke from a cigarette is not the same as the smoke from a wood stove. It makes me sick. I had to take a shower right away. I couldn't do anything with that smell in my nose. I hung my clothes in the bathroom for the air to clean them.

I showed Ricky the cigarette. Don't you know you can die if you smoke these? I said.

We're all going to die, he said. The world's going to blow up.

These were the kinds of things he said. I never had an answer for it.

I started to see he's like my father. He can get angry all of a sudden. My father, if he didn't like the food, maybe he'd throw the plate across the room. It would break into a thousand pieces against the wall. You didn't know, you didn't see it was coming. Or if you came into the house wearing shoes. In Costa Rica automatically you know you're not supposed to walk into a house with shoes. The owner maybe will tell you it's okay, but everything is very nice and clean and you won't feel good if you mess it up. You leave the shoes behind the door. But once my father had a guest from another country and he didn't know this. My father smiled and said come in, don't worry about the shoes, and so the man came in. And then my father was angry. He stopped smiling. After five minutes he told the guest you have to leave now, I'm very busy. The man looked very surprised, because my father had invited him to come. I was sorry for him, but not too sorry. He should know this. If you're going to travel to another country, you have to find out what the tradition is over there. My father didn't stop talking about it for many days.

Ricky also had a temper like that.

One day I took him shopping to buy some shirts. He had no clothes to wear in the winter. I want American shirts, he said. Because already after one month he was starting to like only things that are American. American clothes, American music, American food. If he saw me making cheese like I used to make in Costa Rica, he said why are you making that? Why don't you make American food?

I like this, I said.

You like, he said. This is America. He banged his hand

against the counter so the dishes shook. This is fucking America, he shouted.

You don't have to eat it, I said.

I won't, he said. I only eat American food now.

He ordered a pizza to come to the apartment, and I had to pay for it when it came. I told the man I don't want this, I don't even eat pizza, but he checked his paper and said somebody here ordered it. I told Ricky next time I'm not paying, but I never knew when he was going to call and order. And then what do you say when the man is standing at your door with a pizza, tapping his shoe and waiting for his money? So I had to pay. I didn't want trouble.

Ricky left the pizza box on the counter. He ate cold pizza for breakfast. The cheese on top was like plastic.

When I said we'll go shopping for shirts, he didn't want me to go with him. But I said if you want me to pay, I'm coming with you.

Don't wear that, then, he said. You look like a street lady.

I looked down at my T-shirt. It had some small holes along the bottom, like maybe a mouse chewed at it. I thought what difference does it make, nobody will care about my shirt. I tucked it into my jeans. But then before we left the apartment I changed to a different one. We took the bus.

At the store Ricky was in a good mood. He whistled a little bit while he looked through the racks of shirts. He was a good whistler. Not like me. My father knew music, but I can never even make a tune. He picked out four shirts and went to try them on. I stood outside the door of the changing room.

When he came out with the first one, I looked at him.

The shirt was yellow. It looked good on his dark skin. He's a good-looking boy, I thought. It was the first time I saw it. If he will let his hair grow a little bit he'll be a handsome man. Why not? His father was very handsome. And my own father was.

That's nice, I said. It looks good on you.

It's too big, he said.

It looks good to me, I said.

Then all of a sudden he was angry. His eyes were long and angry. I didn't understand what I saw there.

I look like an asshole, he said. I know what you're thinking.

What am I thinking?

You want me to look like an asshole. Your asshole son with the ugly lip.

Don't be ridiculous, I said.

I'm not stupid. You didn't want me to come here.

You don't know what you're talking about.

Talk English, he said.

People in the store turned to look at us. One woman walked past and put her hands over her ears. You have a problem? I said to her, but she kept walking. I wanted to trip her.

Take off the shirt and let's get out of here, I said to Ricky. I grabbed the other three shirts and started to walk to the door.

You gonna pay for those shirts? Ricky called in English, loud.

I felt my face get hot. I'm doing that, I said. I was so angry I almost forgot. They would think I was trying to steal something. I turned around and went to the counter.

My hands were shaking, and I couldn't find the right money. In my father's church they used to say if you need a ten-colón coin and you can find only a five, that's a sign God is angry with you. I had to pay some of it with pennies. I counted them out from my change bag. There was a long line of customers waiting. An American man and his wife were behind me.

I don't believe these people, the man said.

Most of them don't even bother to learn English, the woman said.

Damn gringos, I said to myself. And my son too.

When we got on the bus, I threw the shirts in his lap. Here. Enjoy it. He didn't say anything.

But when we were almost to the apartment he pulled them out of the bag to touch them. These I like, he said. These are good shirts. His voice was like nothing happened. It was just like my father. After he threw the plate, he would take out his ocarina. After he hit you, he would help you get up. Come on, what's the matter? he'd say. Nothing, you'd say. Because he was right. It wasn't really something. His hand was strong on your arm, helping you stand.

So it was like living with my father again. You walk softly in the house. You think before you say something. You don't want to make him angry. You're afraid what he looks like when he's angry. The blood rises in his face like the red in a thermometer. You're afraid what he can do.

It was the same but it was not the same. Because a father is a father. It's good for a child to be afraid of her father. The other way is not so good.

It was a few months after Shyla was born. I didn't nurse her. Eddie said it's good for the baby, but I never nursed my children. If you nurse you can never be away from them. I remember one of my cousins in Costa Rica was nursing her son until he was two years old. He had all his teeth already. And one time the milk wasn't coming fast enough for him so he bit her. Then when he swallowed he screamed. Because instead of milk his mouth was filled with blood.

Two, three months after Shyla was born I had the red flag back again. I didn't expect it this soon. With Miguel it was six months before I had to worry about that. With Ricky I don't remember. I think even longer. I went to the drugstore to buy Kotex. They sell the very big boxes there.

The drugstore is always a place you find a lot of kids. They have two video machines inside by the door. That day there were maybe five or six kids standing around, playing the games, talking and laughing. I started to walk through the turning door into the store. All of a sudden I saw Ricky. He was facing away from me, but I knew it was Ricky because he was bigger than the other ones. His shoulders, his neck. Next to him they looked like nothing. There was a small boy with red hair who came only to Ricky's chest.

Most of them were American. They were talking English. Ricky too. He said something in English and they all laughed. He laughed. His laugh was like my father's, big and loud. Because when he wasn't angry, my father could be a fun man. He took us on picnics. When he laughed he made other people laugh also, even if they didn't hear the joke. People liked to be with him. He had many friends.

You wanna hang out or go? one of the boys asked.

Let's go, the small boy said.

I'm not done here, Ricky said. He leaned close to the video machine. It made crazy noises, beeps and bangs and little screams.

When you gonna be done, Ricky?

I don't know. I didn't win nothing yet. I want to win.

I'm going, the boy said.

Ricky looked up from the screen. Your mama calling you, Buddy?

No. I just don't want to stay here no more.

His mama wants him home, Ricky said. He poked the smaller boy. You do everything your mama tells you?

She's by herself, Buddy said. She got nobody except me.

Mama's boy, Ricky said.

The other boys said no kidding and Buddy can't even take a piss without asking his mama. Buddy's face was red like his hair. She got nobody, he said. They were all laughing.

I didn't go into the drugstore. I wasn't going to go past them with a big box of Kotex. I kept walking through the turning door out of the store. Ricky didn't see me. I could still hear him laughing when I left the store. It stayed with me for a long time, bouncing off the walls inside my head. When I closed my eyes I could hear it.

What's the matter? Eddie said that night. Because that's how it was with us. He knew about me. Some things he didn't know, I never told him. But he knew when something was right or something was wrong.

He was sitting on the couch. Shyla was on a blanket by his feet, and he was playing a game with her. He made shadows on the wall with his fingers. A dog, a rabbit. I watched him, the square shape of his fingers, the freckles on his arms that run together like countries on a map. It was all familiar to me.

What's the matter? he said again.

He made the rabbit hop across the wall. Its ear moved. Shyla smiled and reached out her hand. I heard once some doctors said babies don't smile because they're happy, it's only gas. But Eddie played this game with Shyla when she was just a month old, and she smiled at him. In this world people don't know anything.

I had a rabbit once, I said.

It's him, isn't it? he said. You're thinking about him.

I didn't answer.

These days it's always him, he said.

Tell me about the toy box, I said. How big is it?

It's big enough.

I started to say where are we going to put this toy box,

but then the front door to the apartment slammed and Ricky came in. I turned to look at him.

Where were you? I said. I thought I could smell cigarette smoke on him.

Out.

Don't you have homework? How are you going to pass the sixth grade if you don't do work?

Leave me alone, he said.

He went to the refrigerator and took out white bread, peanut butter, and some egg salad that was Eddie's. He put the peanut butter on one piece of bread. Egg salad on the other one. He smoothed it with the knife. Then he closed up the sandwich and cut it in two pieces, very neat.

Eddie watched him. That's disgusting, he said. You're a goddamn pig, you know that?

Ricky didn't say anything. He started to go to his room.

Don't take food in there, I said. There will be ants.

He kept walking.

I don't care, I said to myself. All day I'm working, cleaning other people's houses. What he does in his room, I don't care. My own room is clean. I never saw an ant in my room.

Then he stepped over Shyla.

Eddie sat up straighter on the couch. Don't touch her, he said.

Ricky stopped. What?

Don't touch the baby, Eddie said. I don't want you touching her.

I didn't touch her.

Your foot touched her. I saw it. Just leave her alone.

What the hell, Ricky said.

He put his foot on Shyla's head. Eddie stood up.

If you don't want nobody touching her, why don't you keep her at your place? Ricky said. This isn't a fucking nursery school.

Watch it, Eddie said.

I felt the muscles all over my body getting tighter, like screws tightening my bones.

Eddie, I whispered.

Ricky took his foot away. Shyla started to cry.

Get out of here, Eddie said, not looking at Ricky. Just get out.

I'm going, Ricky said.

He walked past us to the little room, carrying his sandwich. I heard him eating behind the curtain.

This is crazy, Eddie said. I can't live like this.

Shyla was still crying on the floor. We stood there, one on either side of the blanket.

She's crying, he said.

I can hear.

So why don't you do something? Pick her up.

She's your baby too.

He didn't move. I couldn't let her cry. I bent down and picked her up.

Did you see how he stepped on her? Eddie said.

He didn't hurt her, I said. He wouldn't hurt her.

Goddamn it, Gloria, are you stupid or just blind? Why don't you send him back to Costa Rica? He doesn't belong here.

My mother won't take him, I said.

Send him to the army, then. They'll take him.

I don't know, I said. He's not even fourteen.

In the army they take anyone, Eddie said. A boy fourteen can also kill.

I don't know, I said again.

I tell you, something has to happen. I can't take much more of this.

He kicked his boot at the wall. Little pieces of plaster crumbled onto the floor. See that? he said. This place is falling apart.

• • •

The next day when I got home from work, I saw balls of fire falling from the window of my apartment to the sidewalk. I ran upstairs. Ricky was making airplanes out of paper. He lit them on fire and threw them out the window.

What the hell do you think you're doing? I screamed.

It's a war.

Good, I said. I'm sending you to the army.

He didn't turn around. There was a scratching sound as he lit another match. He lit them against his fingernail. The nail on his thumb was burnt brown along the edge.

You'll set the whole place on fire, I said.

I grabbed the match and crushed it in my hand. Ricky turned. I didn't move. We stood staring at my fingers, like we were waiting for them to turn into flames.

It was funny. I didn't feel anything when the fire touched my skin. Only later I felt it. A small circle of burnt skin, like a round coin in my palm.

10

He wasn't always like this. When he was a little boy he was very sweet. He had dark curly hair. People used to say such nice hair, where did he get a head of hair like that? But I knew it was from my father. When Ricky woke up in the morning, there was a place on the back of his head where the hair twisted up like a bird's nest.

Can he talk? people said. Because he was four or five years old and he wouldn't talk if people were there. It was because of his lip. Sometimes he said a word wrong, and they didn't understand him. But at home he talked. To me, to my mother. I understood everything he said.

If he had a cookie and he took a bite out of it and then it fell on the floor, I had to give him another one with a bite in it. If I tried to give him another whole cookie, he wouldn't eat it.

We lived in my mother's house, and she took care of them. Because I left the house every day to work in the store, but she didn't leave. If she went out it was just to buy sugar or to visit a neighbor or a relative. All the relatives lived very close in one block, aunts, uncles, cousins. After they finished their cleaning in the morning, the women would go visiting from house to house. Someone visits one aunt, someone visits another aunt. There was no set time for it. If she says I'll come at one o'clock, maybe she'll come at two or three. They had coffee and cake. They drink a lot of coffee over there. The children played together.

My mother liked to visit. She liked to gossip and find out what this one and the other one were doing. But she never stepped out of the streets of the town. She was afraid of the country. She was afraid of wild animals. That's why when my father left to move to the farm she didn't come with us. She never came to see us there.

I told my mother the animals are afraid of people, they don't come out to attack you, and my brothers told her, but she wouldn't listen to what we said. Her mouth was pressed into a thin white stripe, and she turned her face away. She can be a very stubborn woman.

So to see her when we were children, we had to go to her. Sometimes on Sunday afternoon we'd go. If there wasn't a picnic. My father liked to invite people for a picnic after church. We went in the jeep. In Costa Rica most people don't have a car, but my father had. We climbed in and rode through the country with the wind blowing our hair. Sometimes he let my brothers drive. They learned very young. Ten, eleven years old they were driving around the farm. We drove until my father found a place in the hills he wanted to stop. He spread a blanket on the grass and took out meat and cheese and fruit and his ocarina. I lay back on the blanket and felt the music in my bones.

Or he drove to where the *mangles* grow. *Mangle* is a bush that grows between the ocean and the earth. It stands up from the water on roots like legs. There's three kinds. When you cut it, you get a juice like molasses. Maybe thicker than molasses, like a glue. It's against the law to cut it, but people do. Because you can get a lot of money for the *mangle* juice. They use it for the floors. If you have *mangle* on your floors, you can walk there with shoes and nothing will happen to it.

My father loved the *mangle* groves. It made him angry that people cut the trees.

These are men who think nothing of the future, he said. Their children and grandchildren. Someday they'll wake up and look around and see there's nothing left.

He stepped into the water up to his knees to touch the roots.

But sometimes after church my father went to his room and closed the door, and those were the days I went to my mother's house. It was a long walk. Sometimes one brother or another one came with me, but not too much. We work hard all week, we need to rest, they said if I asked. So I went by myself. I carried water in a small container. Then many years later I moved in there. My sons grew up in my mother's house and she was like a mother to them. She combed Ricky's hair every morning, to get the knots out.

He had a wooden wagon he liked to sit in. He pulled it around the square yard behind the house, and inside the house. He put a blanket inside to make it comfortable. Some days he wouldn't get up from the wagon even to eat. We had to bring him his food in there.

He played with Miguel. Ricky made the games and they

played them. They liked to go fishing. After it rained they tied string to a stick and hung them in the puddles. People would pass by and see them standing with their shorts and dirty knees, and they smiled and asked did you catch something yet? Ricky and Miguel giggled and didn't answer.

Sometimes they fought, because they're boys and boys fight, but it wasn't big things. A scratch, or maybe once or twice a black eye. When my mother got a little black-and-white TV for the kitchen, they fought about watching it. Ricky pushed Miguel and Miguel fell and his shoulder snapped out. I had to snap it back in. He screamed like I was murdering him. But these are things that happen. I told Ricky you sit there and think about what you did.

One day I was helping my mother in the house, sifting the rice. You had to sift it before you can cook it, to check for bugs or dirt or little stones. There was a big bucket of rice on the floor between us.

We didn't want the boys in the kitchen. They would play rough, maybe knock over the bucket. So I gave each one a candy and sent them outside. Don't come in here, I said. And don't leave this block. If you leave, I'll send the bad man after you. I used to tell them that to make them behave. Ricky asked me where does the bad man live, and I said under the bed. So they never played by the beds.

We sat on the floor, not talking. I wasn't thinking anything, just feeling the hard brown rice slip between my fingers into the pot on my lap. Outside, you could hear them running and laughing. They were playing horses. They galloped back and forth across the yard.

The sun came in through the window and made the top of

my head warm. My eyes started to close. The rice hitting the pot was like rain at night on the metal roof. Then my mother said, I haven't heard the children for a while.

Just that minute Ricky came to the doorway. Come quick, he said.

What did I tell you? I said. Didn't I say not to come in here until I call you?

I thought he wanted to show me how fast he gallops.

No, he said. He came up next to me and pulled on my shirt. Miguel is dead.

I jumped up. Rice spilled over the floor. I ran out to the yard. My mother was behind me.

Miguel was standing in the middle of the yard. His face was purple, almost black. His eyes were white.

Oh, Jesus, I said.

My mother screamed.

Once when I was a child I held my breath until I could feel my face turn purple. The pain in my chest was like a knife that reached to every part of my body, cutting me apart. I wanted to know what would happen. I wanted to know what my father would do.

Do something, Ricky yelled. Mama, do something.

In one second I was by Miguel. With one hand I picked him up by his ankles and held him upside down, like a naked chicken. With the other hand I hit him on his back as hard as I could. There was a popping sound. The piece of candy flew out of his mouth into the grass.

I felt weak. I almost dropped him. What's the matter with you? I shouted. Can't I even trust you with a piece of candy?

He was coughing like he would never stop.

Don't yell at him, Ricky said.

I stopped. I'm not yelling, I said.

Your mama's frightened, my mother said.

Miguel started to cry. I put my arms around him. It's okay, I said. You're okay.

I rocked him back and forth in the grass. The movement ran through my body and into the ground and I was a little girl again. My father slapped my face. There was the sound of his hand hitting my jaw. He had to do it. Because I wouldn't open my mouth to breathe. In school I told them my brother hit me with a pig's bladder. They used to fill them with rocks and use them for weapons. If it hit you on the face, it could leave a green bruise like that.

I opened my mouth. The air rushed in like water.

Is he dead? Ricky asked.

I came back then. No, I said. You did good.

I love him, Ricky said. He stood with his hands in his pockets.

I wonder if all children are born good. And then some change. Or are some people born with something bad inside them, like a splinter in the heart waiting to come out? It could be that way. A blessing or a curse. What happened to that little boy?

CHAPTER

11

One morning in the winter I was coming home from the supermarket. I prefer to shop in the morning, very early, before it's crowded. I always hate places that are crowded. I like the big empty store with the floors still shiny with wax because nobody walked on them yet. You can move very quick up and down the aisles, taking what you need off the shelves. I push the baby carriage in there and the wheels slide smooth and easy across the floor. Shyla likes that.

And they're not too busy to get you something. You have bananas that are green? I asked the man, and he went to the back to get them. Because I like to buy some that are green, some that are yellow. That's how they should sell them. If you buy them all yellow, they turn rotten before you can eat them. I like fruit, but you can't eat more than one banana.

In Costa Rica they have some grocery stores. You can get things in boxes and things in cans like you get over here. You can buy powdered milk and mix it with fresh milk and cream to pour over a cake. It's called a three-milk cake. And you can buy jars of baby food. But my mother always made all the food for Ricky and Miguel herself. That way it's fresher. She cooked fruits and vegetables and mashed it up for them.

The supermarket here has too much food. A hundred fruits, even when it's not the right time for them, a hundred kinds of apple juice, a hundred boxes of cereal. It makes me dizzy. Who can eat all this food? So I always buy the same few things. For myself I don't need a lot. Only for Shyla will I make food, because she is a little baby. But when Ricky started living here, I had to buy more. More drinks, more bread. He eats more than twenty men on the farm. During the year, the school gave him breakfast and lunch, and I told him eat as much as you can over there because I pay for part of it. But he said he was still hungry. When he came home, he went first to the kitchen. He's like a dog smelling where I keep the food.

If I buy cookies for Shyla, he finishes them. I don't see him do it, but then when I reach my hand into the box it is empty. Just some paper wrappers and some crumbs. He never throws away the box. He leaves it standing on the shelf, like there's still something to eat in there, so I don't know until I come to get one. I say Shyla do you want a cookie? And then I have to tell her sorry, no cookie. Ricky ate your cookie. Two or three times a week I have to go to the supermarket to buy back again what Ricky finished.

Sometimes I buy yogurt and make cheese. It's a soft, white cheese, you can't find it in this country. Shyla likes this cheese. She puts it on everything, her hands, her face, her hair. After she eats I have to scrub her all over with a wash-cloth. She screams and tries to kick me. But I have to rub hard to get her clean.

Shyla will eat meat or something like that if Eddie cooks it. One day this summer he made fish. I came home and there were two small fish with gold skins, lying head to tail on the plate. He peeled back the skins and poked the white meat with a fork.

It's good, he said. I got one for you too.

No, thank you, I said.

Try it. Aren't you even going to try it?

I can't believe he thought I would eat that fish. Their yellow eyes stared up at the ceiling, wet and cold.

I put one of my schoolbooks between us on the table.

I can't look at them, I said.

You're being silly. I grew up on these fish.

He put a piece in his mouth and chewed it. Then he took it out and put it in Shyla's mouth.

What are you doing? I said.

You have to be careful of the bones, he said.

That's disgusting. There's germs.

Do you want her to choke? Look, she loves it.

I couldn't say anything more. Because I saw he was right. When he stopped giving it to her, she patted him with her hand to ask for more. I stood watching her lick the pieces off his fingers. Something twisted inside me.

Eddie doesn't even know how to change a diaper, I thought.

Fine, I said. You feed her, then.

He looked at me. What's the matter with you?

Nothing, I said.

I went into the bedroom. I sat on the bed and turned on the radio. Why doesn't he just take her? I thought. And they can take Ricky. I will live here by myself.

I knew it was silly. But I kept thinking that way. I don't need them, I thought. I don't need anyone.

Gloria? Eddie called, but I pretended I couldn't hear him through the radio.

When I came out of the bedroom a short time later, Shyla was sleeping in Eddie's lap. Eddie was also asleep. His chin was resting on her head. The fish was gone. All that was left on the plate were the eyes and two piles of small white bones.

• • •

That morning I wasn't in the supermarket very long. There was just one woman in line in front of me, with a little boy. She was buying two cartons of eggs and maybe thirty lemons. I thought what can you do with eggs and lemons? Shyla was fussy. I told her be quiet, we're almost done here, but she didn't stop. The woman looked at me. Her boy was quiet. He was eating a candy she gave him from the boxes near the cash register. I wanted to say candy is bad for children. I don't give my baby candy. If I gave her candy she'd also be quiet like that.

The woman needed two bags for all those lemons. My own things came to only one bag. I never get more than one bag because I don't like to carry it. I know exactly how much food makes one bag of groceries. I put it in the bag myself while the girl was doing the cash register. That way it's faster. Thanks for bagging, she said. Sometimes they're polite like that.

When I came out of the store, I saw the woman with the

lemons was still there. She was putting the boy in the little car they have by the door. You drop in some coins and it gives the kids a ride.

I never let Shyla ride that car. Once I saw a rat go in there. When I saw it, I went back into the supermarket and told the man there's a rat on your ride.

I doubt that, he said.

Yes, I said. I saw it.

We don't have rats here, he said, and he walked away.

So now I told the woman it's a dangerous ride.

Worry about your own kid, why doncha? she said. Her nose's running.

I looked at Shyla. All babies get a runny nose when they cry. It doesn't mean I'm a bad mother. I reached into my pocket like I'm getting a tissue, but I knew there was no tissue there. I never carry a tissue with me. When the woman turned away, I wiped Shyla's nose with my finger. I squeezed my bag of groceries next to her in the carriage.

It wasn't even eight o'clock when I started walking home. I sang a song to Shyla in Spanish about the rabbit and the fox, but she didn't stop crying. Fine, I said. Cry if you want to cry. Then when I was almost at my street I heard a siren behind me. A fire truck went by. You see, I said. He's coming to get you because you're a bad girl.

When I came to the street, I saw it was blocked. There were orange cones with yellow tape across, and they weren't letting people come in there. The fire truck was parked by the curb in front of my building.

Sorry, the officer said. He had big black rubber boots. You'll have to go a different way.

I live here, I said.

Which building?

I told him.

That's where it is, he said. Right in front there.

Inside my jacket I was cold all over. My knees felt like air.

He didn't mean it, I said. He's crazy. He thinks it's a war.

The officer stared at me. Who? he said.

I told him, I said. I told him Ricky you'll put the building on fire and burn us down in our beds.

There's no fire, the officer said. Some kids opened the hydrant.

Then I saw the water, pouring at me down the street. It rushed along the curbs with a loud sucking noise. The street was turning to a dirty river while I watched. Pieces of newspaper and empty cans floated on top of the water.

No fire, I said. It was like a heavy package was lifted away from me. But then I thought of something else. What kids? I asked the officer.

I wish I knew. I'd wring the bastards' necks. They must've been up pretty early, though.

Oh, I said.

It was okay. Ricky hates to get up early.

I couldn't get the carriage through. I stood on the corner for almost an hour while they waited for the water to go down. I kept looking at my watch. I'll be late for work, I thought. It was Brenda's day, and she was having a party. I needed all the time there, because of the broken vacuum. It took longer to clean. But after the time passed that I usually leave, I stopped worrying about it because I was already late.

I couldn't feel the tops of my fingers, or my toes. I closed my hands into knots in my pockets to try to keep warm. The sewers were clogged. The firemen walked around, shouting different things I didn't hear or didn't understand.

When I finally got to my building, I looked up at the window. I tried to see was there a light on in there, but the sun shone off the glass and I couldn't see anything. I went upstairs. I put my keys in the lock and it stuck and nobody came to the door to open it. There was no noise inside the apartment. He's still asleep, I thought.

But when I got inside he was there, awake. He was standing by the window, already dressed. He had jeans with very big legs. You could fit three of me into each one of those legs.

I was sick all over. What are you doing up? I said.

I couldn't sleep. Because of the noise.

Did you see what happened out there? I said. I knew it was a stupid question, he's not blind, but I had to say something. I thought he'd answer back something nasty, but he just said I see. I couldn't tell anything from his voice. He was still looking out the window.

You can't stand there all day, I said. You have school.

I'm going.

Did you go outside yet? I asked. But then I wished I didn't ask it. I started talking right away so he couldn't answer me.

It took me an hour to come home. It's cold out. Very cold. You better take a jacket.

I started to put away the groceries. He came away from the window. When he passed the table, he reached into the grocery bag and took out a whole loaf of bread. He left the apartment, tearing pieces from the bread and pushing them into his mouth. He didn't have a jacket.

I'm not making any supper, I called after him. You want food, you take. There's chicken in the freezer.

I picked up a box of animal crackers and put it far back on the shelf, behind some paper towels. Maybe he wouldn't find it over there. I called Brenda to tell her I'll be very late for work.

Something happened with my son, I said.

What happened?

Nothing, I said. I thought it was something.

Well, please try to hurry, she said. My guests are coming at one. I count on you to be here on time.

When I came outside the fire truck was gone. I went to work. I had to work very fast to finish and I dropped something, a glass holder with a tall pink candle inside that hung on the wall in the dining room. I was afraid to pick it up and see if it was cracked. How could I tell her I broke her candle? I stood a long time before I picked it up.

It wasn't broken. But I knew I was just lucky. It could happen again. My hands, I notice, aren't as careful these days as they used to be. It makes me afraid. Next time maybe I won't be so lucky.

CHAPTER

12

I still say boys are easier, Jackie said. We were in her apartment after church. Jackie was putting color in her hair. She said it makes nice highlights in the summer. She stood in front of the bathroom mirror, and I sat on the toilet, watching.

It says red, she said, looking at the box. But I don't know. She squeezed some onto her finger. What do you think?

To me it looked purple. But I said yes, it's red.

The picture shows red, she said.

It's red, I told her.

She already bought it and she wanted red. If I said it was purple she'd never use it. That's how she is.

When I was pregnant with Shyla, the doctor said do you want to know if it's a boy or a girl, and I said no, I don't want. Because I already have two boys, I thought a girl will be nicer. I can tie a little bow in her hair. But Jackie said trust me, you don't know what you're saying. She hung a needle on a string and put it over my stomach to see if it will swing straight or in a circle. It went in a circle. What does that mean? I said.

I can't remember, she said. I think it means a girl. But maybe I'm wrong.

Jackie is a good friend. She's the one who first brought me to the church. When I moved here, she knocked on my door the next day. I'm your neighbor, she said. I brought you a little something. It was a white cake and a small Bible.

She asked me do you have religion? I said my father was a Catholic, but I hadn't gone to church in eleven years. She told me there's a special group, and she invited me to go with her. She said they get together every Monday night and they learn everything there.

So I went to the group and talked to them. It was in a woman's home. She had coffee and doughnuts. Everyone sat in a circle, some on chairs and some on the floor. It was all Hispanic people. They read the Bible. They talked about their problems with work and everything else.

One man who worked in a diner said a woman there asked for decaf coffee. But when he brought it she didn't believe it was decaf. He got angry and said things to her, and she complained to the manager. The next day he was fired.

It always happens this way, he said. Every time I swear it won't happen again. The customer's always right, no matter what. But then it happens again.

He lost three jobs, his wife said. We have a two-year-old and a newborn.

The man looked around the circle. The skin on his face was soft and loose. It was a good face. There were things there that I understood.

It's like something outside yourself, he said. Like the devil comes into you and takes you over and it's not you who's saying it or doing it.

People nodded. Then somebody said let's pray, and we held hands and prayed.

After the meeting, I went over to the man. I'm sorry about your job, I said.

Me too, he said. He smiled. I'm Victor.

He held out his hand, and I put my own hand in it. His hand was big and soft. I kept my fingers there for a minute.

I'm Gloria. I came over here from Costa Rica.

Welcome to our little family. I hope you'll come back to us.

I don't know, I said. It's not easy for me to come at night.

But I did come back. I saw what they did, how they practiced. They don't eat a lot of meat. They don't drink wine. I liked this. I started going every week. After that, I never missed it.

Each time it was at a different house. Sometimes I brought Shyla with me. Other women also brought their children. They slept together on the bed. Their arms and legs were tangled together like one big animal.

A few times they came here. I put out cheese and crackers, nothing fancy. Coca-Cola or orange Fanta in plastic cups. But since Ricky came I didn't have them. I never knew when I came into the apartment if he would be there or not. I didn't want them here when he was here. I told him this is my religion, this is what I do. You don't bother me and I won't bother you. But I didn't know what he would say if he saw people sitting around in a circle, holding hands and praying. I didn't know what they would say if they saw him.

Jackie drew a line on her head with the comb and put some color there. She left it for a short minute, then combed it into her hair. Her hair is black like mine, but shorter, just to the ears, and it curls at the ends.

I passed the bedroom yesterday, she said, and I heard my two girls talking. And you know what she said? The little one? She said so then he asked me do I want to have sex with him. I stopped breathing. She's only eight years old. I didn't know she knew the word.

Of course they know, I said. What do you think?

I smelled the color across the bathroom. It smelled like clay.

She drew another line on her head, and another one. The skin under her hair was very white.

I went in there and I said what are you two talking about, and they said nothing. And I said it didn't sound like nothing to me. So the other one said we're talking about sex and they giggled.

That's how it is, I said. It's what they see and what they hear.

I know, she said. She leaned closer to the mirror. Do you know I found two gray hairs? I'm getting old. Children make you old.

She sighed. I didn't know what to say to them. I said I don't know what you two know and what you don't know, but you start fooling around how you shouldn't and you'll be sorry. Aw, we're just talking, she said. So what do you do? You can't watch them every second.

It's not your fault, Jackie, I said. You can't blame yourself for it.

I'm their mother. I thought maybe I'll get rid of the TV, but then they'll just go to a friend's house to watch.

It's not only TV, I said. Even at the bus station you see it. You can't do anything.

I pray, she said. That's why I go to church.

She turned around to face me and held up the tube of color.

I have some left. Why don't I do you next?

I don't have gray hair, I said. Not yet.

You can have some anyway, she said. It goes good with your skin.

But I said no. Save it for Michaela.

Right now Michaela's not getting anything from me, she said.

Jackie was always trying to make me look fancy. She wanted to take me to the department store. They have counters with red stools and swinging mirrors that make your face look big. You can see every pimple there. The women wait behind the counters with their lipsticks and powders and little brushes. When you walk past, they call honey do you have a minute? Give me five minutes, you'll see what I can do for you. Once I went by and one of them said that one looks like she can use a little something. Maybe they thought I couldn't hear them or I didn't understand, but I understood what they were saying about me. I hate it when they call you honey.

We'll let them do your face, Jackie said. Just to see.

You know I don't wear makeup, I told her.

You don't have to buy anything, she said. Just to see how it looks. Men like it if you wear a little makeup.

I'm not looking for men, I said. Eddie doesn't care about this.

It's true what I told her. When Eddie first started coming upstairs, I used to put on a nice shirt, maybe wash my hair. He knocked twice and said it's me, Eddie, like I didn't know. Who else would it be at night? I looked in the mirror before I opened the door. But then I saw if I wash it or I don't wash it he doesn't notice. So I stopped doing it. How I am, I am. It's better that way. You know there's no tricks behind it. With some men, there's always a trick.

I once asked him do men like lipstick? He said some like it, some don't.

Do you like it? I said.

He shrugged. I don't like when it comes off on the cups, he said.

I didn't know about sex until I was married, Jackie was saying. What about you?

I was never married, I said.

No kidding. I didn't know that. I just thought—we were all married sometime.

Not me, I said.

With Ricky's father it was one month, maybe two months. He was my father's worker. And with other men less. With Miguel's father, it was one night, a man without a place passing through the town. Your luck, my mother said, to have a body that makes a baby in one night.

Jackie looked at me in the mirror. Her mouth was crooked. Are you going to marry Eddie? she asked.

No. I don't see a reason for it.

Why not? You like each other, don't you? You have a kid.

You don't need to be married to have a kid. You don't need to be married for sex. You don't need to be married for anything. It's just something they tell you.

The church says you should be married.

My father was married to my mother for thirty-five years. It didn't make a difference.

Well, anyway, that's your business, she said. But they're only eight and twelve. They shouldn't know about these things.

She held out the tube again. It's your last chance.

I shook my head.

She turned on the sink and stuck her head under to rinse it. Praying works, she said through the water. Once I missed a month and when I realized it the first thing I did was start praying. Two days later I got it. Did you try praying about Ricky?

I said maybe I'll do that.

I wanted to see how Jackie's hair would turn out, but she said you have to wait until it dries and that will be maybe an hour, because she doesn't have a hair dryer. She says it ruins your hair. And I didn't want to stay another hour. I had done enough talking, I wanted to be in my own apartment. But the next time I saw her, Monday night at the Bible meeting, I looked at her hair. First it looked red, but when she stood by the light I saw it was purple.

Do you like it? she asked me.

It looks good, I said.

At that meeting I told them I want to pray for my son. And every night after that when I got into bed I put the blanket over my head like a tent, and in the dark space underneath, where it smells of sleep, I asked God to show me what to do with him. I waited for a sign. In my father's church they said if you need to go outside and it rains that's also a sign from God. So even though I don't have that religion anymore, I believe this. There's parts of it that stay with you. I remembered it was raining when Ricky came here.

CHAPTER 13

There are some things you don't forget. You grow up and have a child and another child and change your country and change your religion and a piece of you is still back there. You close your eyes and you can see it and smell it like it's happening now.

I remember when I was maybe ten years old, my father made a party for some of his friends at the house. I was asleep. All of a sudden I felt someone shaking my arm. It was his new girlfriend, Juana. Get up, she said. Her rings scratched my cheek. Your father wants to see you. She handed me my best dress, red velvet with a white lace collar. Here, put this on. Hurry.

I didn't want to go. I was very tired. My arms and legs felt like wood. And I could hear the crowds of people out there, talking and laughing. My throat closed with tears. But I got up and put on the dress.

The house smelled like pretty women. My father was

playing his ocarina by the fireplace, and someone else was playing a guitar. A woman was singing. She had a tight black dress and bare shoulders. My father watched her while he played. His foot tapped against the floor. I stood in the doorway and waited for him to see me.

The music was very lively. The man with the guitar played good, but not perfect. He made some mistakes. All of a sudden a note scratched. My father didn't mind this. He always invited people who weren't perfect to play with him. There's more spirit in the music, he said.

He liked only simple instruments. The guitar, the marimba, the ocarina. The ocarina is very simple, like an egg with holes for your fingers. My father's was made from clay. I thought it was wonderful. But I knew when he was younger my father wanted a violin.

Once, at a different party, a man came to the house with a violin. He started to set up his music in front of the fire.

We don't need that, my father said. We have enough here without it.

You always need a violin, the man said.

There's no room. Can't you see how crowded it is?

Oh, let's have the violin, the women said.

I could see my father was angry. The muscle in his cheek jumped like a salamander under the skin. He stopped playing his own instrument.

After the party, I was cleaning up the room and my father came in.

A violin does not go with a marimba, he said. Did you hear how bad it sounded?

I nodded.

He is a great show-off, my father said. He wanted to make me look bad in my own house. I don't need such people. His eyes were black clouds. You understand this?

I said yes. I didn't know why the man would want my father to look bad. They used to be friends. When he came to the house, he brought wine and they drank it together from tall glasses. They talked and laughed about things I didn't understand. But I knew if my father said it he must be right. I never saw the man in our house again.

But that night when I stood in the doorway I saw my father was happy. I saw he liked this man with the guitar. He was an older man with a mustache that curled like a black feather. His face was red from working hard, maybe also from wine.

The music stopped. Bravo! someone called. My father stood up and kissed the woman with the black dress on the cheek. She laughed. He laughed.

Here she is, a woman said. The little chef.

People turned to look at me. So many eyes coming at me from so many places. Some of the women had green paint on their eyelids, and it glittered in the light from the fire. I wanted to go back to my bed. I wanted to disappear into the air like smoke.

Your father said you made all the food yourself. These pastries are wonderful.

I was baking for a week. Every night I made another something. Cakes with almonds, tiny pies with coconut, pineapple, and yam. I kept them on trays in the oven because there was no room anyplace else. The pastries were shaped like bow ties. They had chocolate inside and white sugar outside. They were on silver plates carved with birds and flowers.

My father smiled. Isn't she something special? he said.

My cheeks were warm. I felt a tickle like a finger moving down my back.

Here, my father said to me, holding out a plate. Have a pastry.

I could taste the chocolate on my tongue. But I was afraid to take it. I thought I will get chocolate on my nice dress, and he'll be angry, and he won't look at me like that anymore. No, thank you, I said.

He shook his head. What kind of child doesn't like chocolate? Everyone laughed. They were still looking at me. But it wasn't so bad now, because of my father.

Let's have some more music, my father called. I want to dance.

The man with the mustache picked up his guitar. My father took my hand.

I didn't know how to dance. My feet didn't know what to do.

Come on, my father said. Don't just stand there.

I tried to wiggle my hips like I saw the women doing. I felt silly. The different parts of me didn't want to move together. I knew without looking that everyone was watching. My brothers were still asleep. I was the only child.

Just do something, he said. Do anything.

I raised my arms over my head and waved them, like palm leaves moving in the wind.

That's good, he said. He put his hands on my shoulders.

I moved faster. I wasn't tired anymore. I felt the blood running through my body.

The woman in black tapped my father on the shoulder.

He pushed away her hand. Can't you see I'm dancing with my daughter? he said. He grabbed me and spun me around. I was lighter than the tiny pieces of colored dust you could see floating in the air.

He smelled like wine. The flame from the fire lit up his face, and when he looked at me his eyes were proud.

You see? he said. That's the secret. Never just stand there. You have to make like an elephant.

I thought I could dance with him forever. It was the happiest night I remember.

CHAPTER
14

One day in February I woke up and I thought tomorrow is Ricky's birthday. I wanted to get him something, but I didn't know what to get. I asked the woman where I was cleaning what can I buy a boy turning fourteen?

How about a nice wallet? she said.

No. He doesn't need this.

A sweater, maybe?

Not a sweater either. He doesn't like sweaters.

I'm afraid I'm not very helpful, she said. You know my children are all grown. I send them a check.

I thought I can get him more pants. You can always wear pants. He likes them with a lot of pockets. He keeps things there. He always has a plastic comb in his back pocket. He won't go anywhere without this comb. I told him why don't you let your hair grow so you have something to comb, but he pretended he didn't hear me. He has other things too. Money, pens, matches, a piece of clay. I have to remember to check the pockets before I wash something, or who knows what can happen? Once I took out the wash and there was clay on everything. Blue spots on the towels, the underwear. I screamed at him normal people empty their pockets before they put something to be washed, but he said it was my fault. Why don't you check before you put it in the machine? he said.

Pants are not a very good present. When I was a kid, I never liked to get clothes for a present. You have to have clothes. I wanted something different. On our birthdays my father used to reach into your ear and pull out a silver coin. Buy something special, he'd say. Then when you had some time you could walk into town and pick something from the window. Candy or a kite. Or when I got older I just kept the coin. It was better that way. Because chocolate got used up no matter how small you made the bites, and the kite was made from thin sticks and paper and got broken by the wind, but the coin stayed. I would wrap it up in paper and keep it under my pillow for many weeks. Every day I'd take it out to look at it. I felt very rich. I thought I will save these coins and someday I'll take a trip to a beautiful place with a beautiful name, very far away.

He gave us a coin like that every year, except one year, when I was thirteen, he forgot. At breakfast I thought he'll remember at dinner. At dinner I thought before bed. Lying in bed, I thought today he was very busy, he'll remember tomorrow. But he never did. There was a plain yellow cake I baked. I left it in the oven for two days and finally when I saw he wasn't going to remember I cut it into squares and put it on the table after dinner. My father had three pieces. He didn't say anything about it. My brothers gave me a card and that was all.

I don't know what happened to those coins. There were seven, for each year since I started saving minus one. When I left his house, I left in a hurry. There was no time to take them with me.

For Ricky I wasn't thinking to give money. Then I thought of a watch. I knew he didn't have one, and everybody needs a watch. On the way home I stopped at a store to look.

It's for a boy, I told the Indian man at the counter. He had a pink turban with a red stone to hold it closed.

He pulled out a tray with maybe a hundred watches. How about this one? he said, pointing. Very good watch. It's the most popular style now with teenagers.

I picked it up. It was small and light in my palm.

No good, I said. He has a very big hand.

I picked up another one. Black with a leather band.

You like? he said. That is also a good watch. Waterproof, lights up in the dark, everything.

He showed me how the numbers light up green when you touch a button. It looked like a good watch.

How much? I said.

He told me a price.

That's too much.

I tell you something. Because it's a present, I will give you a special price.

It wasn't cheap but I thought Ricky will like it. Okay, I'll take this, I said. He put it in a box.

The next morning I took a long time getting ready for work. I thought maybe Ricky will wake up and I can give

him the watch before I leave. I kept walking past the curtain
to check if I heard noise behind there. I even peeked inside.
Ricky was lying without moving on the cot. It looked to me
like he would never move.

Finally I left the box on the table with a note. I lay Shyla
on the floor and started to put on her things. White snowsuit,
hat, mittens with faces on the fingers. Who would think I'd
have a baby who knows snow? Then he came in.

Happy birthday, I said.

He rubbed his eyes. I'm still sleeping, he said.

I got you a present. It's on the table.

He looked at the box but didn't pick it up.

Hurry up, I said. Open it. I have to go to work.

A watch, he said when he opened the lid.

Do you like it? I tried to see in his face what he was thinking.

I already have a watch, he said.

No, you don't. I never saw you wear a watch.

I wear it. I wear it all the time.

He held out his arm. He was wearing a watch. How can I
not have seen it? It was black also, but the band was plastic.

I never take it off, he said. I sleep with this watch.

I tried to smile. So now you have two.

I don't want it, he said. I don't want two watches.

This new one is nicer, I said. It has a leather band.

I don't want it, he said again.

I was angry. At Ricky, at myself.

Okay, I said, pulling it out of his hand. I'll return it.

It was a week before I went back to the store. It was the
same man at the counter. What's wrong with it? he said. He

took out a pad and a pen. The red stone in his turban glittered.

Nothing. I just don't want it.

I waited for him to give me the money.

I need to write down what's wrong with it, he said. Or else we can't take it back.

Why? I said.

I don't know why. Those are the rules.

I started to tell him it's a stupid rule, but all of a sudden I had enough of it. I didn't feel like fighting. It was for my son, I told him.

He looked at me funny. I understand, he said. I'm so sorry.

He gave me the money. I have a teenage boy myself, he said. I can feel in my heart what you're going through.

I did not understand what he was talking about. I said thank you and left the store. If he thought he knew about Ricky, he didn't know anything.

When I came home, Ricky was lying on the couch with some comic books and the radio playing. Even though it was winter, he was wearing a thin black T-shirt. He didn't move when I came in. I stood looking down at his back. I could see the muscles like long snakes through his shirt.

I don't know why I did it. But I leaned over and held out the money. Here. Buy yourself something.

He sat up. I could see in his face that he couldn't decide about it. Then he took it from me and nodded. *Gracias,* he said.

I watched him fold up the money. I stood there, but he didn't say anything more. I hate that English music he was playing. It's noise, not music.

Just show me what you pick, okay? I said finally. I want to know what I give my son for his birthday.

That night he came to me when I was doing my English homework. We had a workbook that's supposed to teach you things. It had different pages for different things. Like if you're eating in a restaurant, there was a page that said I'd like to order the lobster with peas, with a picture so you can see what it is. You had to put the stickers by the words and then write the sentences. Then there was another page called emergencies. It said my baby swallowed poison, there's smoke coming from the basement, I need an ambulance.

It was not a very good book. Because maybe you don't like lobster. In my religion we don't eat pig and we don't eat lobster. Or maybe there's something else wrong, another kind of emergency, and you can't tell them about it because you don't have the words. But I did the exercises she told us. The teacher then was a different teacher and she didn't check the work. But there's no point to take lessons if you don't do the work. If you don't do it you won't learn.

I was doing the page with different jobs. They had doctor, nurse, policeman, garbage collector. They didn't have my job.

Ricky stood watching me put down the stickers. He leaned over the chair.

That one's a mechanic, he said, pointing where I had left it out. The picture was a little man with some kind of tool.

Mecánico. That's what I'll do. Or else I'll be a cop.

I looked at him, surprised. I didn't know he thought these kinds of things. Just like I didn't know about the watch. This boy is living in my house five months and I don't know him at all, I thought. What he thinks, what he does.

You have to study to be a cop, I said.

I know that, he said.

He reached into his pocket. I got this one. He held it out to me.

It was a pocketknife, very fancy, with a white handle like the inside of a seashell. He moved his thumb up and down the handle.

A knife, I said.

Yes. Isn't she a beauty?

I don't know. Why do you need a knife?

Everyone has. If you don't have a knife, they won't even look at you.

He opened it. The blade glittered.

I didn't know what to say. He shouldn't have a knife. I knew Eddie wouldn't like it that he had one. But I said he could buy whatever he wanted. I can't take it back from him.

When I was maybe eleven, twelve years old my father took away my rag doll. You're too old for dolls, he said. Besides, it's dirty. He said he'd bury it in the yard, and I thought on a morning when he isn't home I'll dig it up. But when I got outside I didn't know where to dig. I stood with a little shovel, staring at the hills of dirt. He came home and found me there. What are you doing?

Nothing, I said.

Do you want to plant something? There's plenty of seeds. Plenty of work.

Okay.

But then he got angry. Girls don't plant, he said. Get back inside.

He wanted to protect me. Planting seeds is hard work. It makes your back crooked. I'll never have a crooked back.

• • •

Ricky was still standing there, waiting for me to say something. A big boy, and strong. And the knife was big. It looked very sharp.

Put it away, I said finally. Before Eddie sees.

He smiled at me. *Gracias,* he said again.

It was the first time I saw him happy. He used to smile sometimes. When he was a little boy, if you touched his feet he smiled. You're tickling me, he said. Even if you didn't touch him, you just came close. He rolled away on the bed, laughing.

It's just a pocketknife, I thought. All the boys have them.

CHAPTER

15

Riding the bus one afternoon, I heard Ricky's voice behind me. First I thought I was imagining it. You listen for something a lot, you start to hear it even when it's not there, even in your sleep. Sometimes I heard him cursing in my dreams. But then it came again. Loud. I had no trouble hearing the words.

Leave him alone, he said.

I turned around, keeping my head down so he won't notice me. The bus was crowded, and I had to look through the people to see him. Ricky was standing a few rows back in the aisle. There were four or five kids with him, all standing. I recognized some of them from the time in the drugstore. I saw Buddy there. He was holding something in a plastic bag.

It's for my mama, he said. For her birthday. My mama likes fish.

I twisted my head to see better. I saw a spot of orange moving inside the bag. It was a goldfish.

What kinda present is that? a boy said.

Fish are for eating, another kid said. He tried to take the bag away from Buddy.

I said leave him alone, Ricky said again. What about that don't you understand?

The kid said something I couldn't hear.

I didn't see what happened next. The bus went over a bump and a woman who was standing in the aisle fell into my lap. I'm sorry, she said. Oh, I'm so sorry.

It's okay, I said.

No, it's my fault, she said, standing. I'm so sorry.

She patted her hair and laughed a small, nervous laugh. It's lucky, she said. These days you never know. A person can take out a gun and shoot you for falling in their lap. For less even.

I smiled. But inside I was thinking shut up, please. I wanted to hear what was happening with Buddy.

Then I heard him scream and Ricky said shit and when I turned around Buddy's hands were empty.

Get him, he was screaming. He gonna die.

He's gone, man, Ricky said.

There's a fish loose, a man called.

Some of the boys laughed. Buddy started to cry.

I looked down at the floor, but I couldn't see the fish there. Other people were also looking. But not everyone. The woman who fell in my lap was sitting in a seat now, reading a magazine. She licked her finger to turn the page, not even picking up her head. It was like she didn't notice anything. Some people the whole world can fall apart around them and they just sit there.

The bus stopped. Ricky came to the front. He was pushing Buddy in front of him. They came past me. I turned my head away to the window.

It's okay, man, Ricky said. We'll get another fish for your mama.

Then they were gone.

I looked out the window to see is there someplace there where you can buy a fish, but I didn't see anything. It was the part of the city where a lot of the stores are boarded up. There's a big building that used to be for roller skating, but they closed it a few months after I moved to the city because kids came there to sell drugs. Before they closed it, I used to pass by on the bus and think Ricky and Miguel would like this place. You could always hear music coming from there.

I thought again how I don't know this boy who is my son.

That night when Ricky came home I said tell me about your friends in Costa Rica. Did you have a lot of friends over there?

I had friends, he said.

What did you do? To have fun?

Why are you asking me these questions? he said.

He turned on the TV, too loud for talking.

Eddie came in later. He stood by the sink, getting ready to cook.

Can't you do something except sit in front of that damn TV? he said to Ricky. Why don't you read a book?

He reached into the sink. There was meat defrosting there, drops of blood coming through the white paper. When he picked up his hands, they were red with blood. I thought I could smell it across the room.

I know what blood smells like. If my father hit you hard

enough, there could be blood. You didn't scream. You never screamed or he hit you harder. You bent down in the dirt next to the giant rock. You didn't move. You didn't think. You went outside yourself. Dirt, rock, sky. The green waves washing up on the sand again and again.

Later you wrapped it in a cloth so it wouldn't drip on the floor. When it healed, there were red stripes across your hand.

Cat scratch you again? my mother said when I came there to visit.

No, I said. I burned myself on the stove.

You should be more careful, she said.

The room was very quiet. Eddie and Ricky were both looking at me. I shook my head.

When's the last time you read a book? I said to Eddie.

He frowned. I work. It's different. Besides, I got some books in the basement.

Well, don't lecture him.

I started to go to my room.

Eddie put down the meat and came across the room. For a minute he stood looking from me to Ricky. Then he picked up his keys from the table. I'm going to get some food. Do you want something?

I thought you were cooking, I said.

I changed my mind.

Oh. No, I don't want anything.

He didn't ask Ricky.

When he was leaving the apartment, I said aren't you going to do something with that meat?

No, he said. If you don't like it, you do something with it.

He didn't come back that night. The meat stayed in the

sink because I didn't want to touch it. But in the morning when it was still there I threw it away. I washed my hands again and again to get the blood off.

• • •

A few nights later I came home and Ricky was taking apart the TV. He said the picture was fuzzy and he could fix it.

I didn't notice anything wrong with the TV, Eddie said when he came into the apartment and saw the pink and green wires spread out on the floor.

Let him do it, I said. He wants to do it.

He had a bag of little tools. I watched how his fingers moved, putting together the wires and tiny screws.

He gets it from me, I thought. This one thing comes from me.

If you break it, there's no more TV, Eddie said. What will you do then?

Shut up, Ricky said. I know what I'm doing.

Eddie didn't leave the room. The whole time Ricky was working he stood over him, like some kind of guard.

Go away, Ricky said.

I guess I can stand here if I want, Eddie said.

Ricky fit it all together again. He knew where everything goes. Afterward, when I turned it on to see my shows, I thought maybe the picture is a little bit clearer.

See, the lines are better, I said to Eddie.

It's no different, he said.

He touched my shoulder. Don't fool yourself, Gloria, he said. Nothing's changed with him. Nothing's going to change.

CHAPTER
16

But in life things are always changing. At work one day I find I have to be a nurse.

I clean for an old man and his wife, Mr. and Mrs. Robison. They are both very sick, but she is more sick, so he tries to take care of her. But he can't do it. One morning I'm there and she asks for some soup. He empties a can of red soup in a bowl and brings it to her in the bed. He doesn't cook it, he doesn't make it hot. I come into the room to open the shade and I see she is eating cold soup. I take the bowl. Let me do it, I say. I will make soup for both of you. I find a little pot and cook the soup, and I stay there with them while they eat. I help her with the spoon. That's nice, she says, closing her eyes.

I start doing things for them. I wash her face and hands with a warm cloth. I turn his chair so it faces the sun. Sometimes before I leave there I make some sandwiches and leave them in the refrigerator. Old people need to eat.

I don't know how to be a nurse. But sometimes you have

to do what you don't know. I feel something here in my heart when I do these things for them.

Once I said to her let me comb your hair. Because I saw it was full of knots. I sat on the side of the bed and took a little piece in my hand. Her hair is very light and thin, like cotton from an old quilt.

That's nice, she said.

I smiled.

Nice. You must be a good mother.

No, I said. I'm no good.

I have a daughter in Chicago, she said. Maureen. But she never visits, she never calls.

She closed her eyes. Her eyelid was thinner than a tissue where the sun shines through. I thought she was asleep.

My father, I said. He knew what to do. He knew how to raise a child.

I would like some Jell-O, she said without opening her eyes.

Jell-O? I tried to think what is Jell-O.

Yes. I haven't had Jell-O in years. My mama used to make it for us when we were sick. It feels so good going down.

Then I knew what it was. Some women make it for their babies. They cut it into little squares and give it to them on the playground. Not me, I never made this Jell-O. To me it is a disgusting food.

But I thought why not, if this is what she wants. The house here is clean and there's nothing waiting for me in my apartment. There's no reason to rush back there.

I will get you Jell-O, I said.

Red, she said when I was leaving. I like red.

I had to go to three stores before I found it. The first place had no Jell-O. The second place had only green and yellow. Are you sure no red? I asked the man.

What you see is what I got, he said. That stuff's been lying around here forever.

But at the third store I bought a box of cherry Jell-O. I brought it back to the house.

You have to leave it in the fridge overnight, Mrs. Robison said. She was excited, like a little girl. She wanted to watch me mix it. I took the bowl into the bedroom so she could see. She stuck her finger in the bowl and licked her finger, and I laughed.

Sometimes they put fruit in it, she said. But it's better without.

I left the bowl on the top shelf in the refrigerator. Don't forget to eat it, I said.

How can I forget? she said.

The next week when I came there I asked them how was the Jell-O?

What?

The Jell-O.

I don't know about any Jell-O, Mr. Robison said. We haven't had Jell-O here for years.

My mama used to make it, Mrs. Robison said. Maybe someday you can make us some Jell-O, Gloria. I like red.

I didn't know what to say. It's terrible to be old. In my country the young people take care of the old people. If your parents are old and sick, you bring them into your house. But here it's not that way. Who will take care of me if I can't work? I don't want to live if I can't work. I don't want to live to be more than sixty.

I looked in the refrigerator for the bowl. It was still there, pushed into the back behind some open cans. Maybe it's still good, I thought. But I was afraid to give it to her. I don't need something happening, I don't need her to get sick. So I threw it away.

CHAPTER
17

In April I went to work and the woman said Gloria, did you see my stockings? This is a house where I was work-ing a long time. No, I said. I didn't see them. Then I forgot about it. I have other things to think about than to worry about her stockings. But in an hour she came to me again. I was cleaning the bathroom, washing the mirrors with vinegar to get the toothpaste off.

Gloria, she said, standing behind me. Those stockings cost me fifty dollars. They're in a box from Macy's.

I didn't see them, I said. But I will look.

It smells like a salad in here, she said.

Her name is Lillian. She's not an easy woman. When you work like I work, you have to know the people. You know which house you can take milk for your coffee, which house you can't. Some places she'll give you lunch, soup or a sand-wich. She'll put down a napkin and sit at the table and talk to you while you eat. Or else she'll say take something when you want it, and then you know you're supposed to eat lunch while you work. Sometimes I eat, sometimes no. But Lillian never gave lunch. If I made coffee, I drank it black without milk. She knew exactly how much was in the carton.

I looked around the bedroom for the stockings. The house isn't so messy. Sometimes if they have little kids you can find a banana peel under the bed or something like that. Once I found a dead turtle. It smelled so bad I almost threw up. I remember that smell of rotting skin from the beaches in my country, when a dead sea turtle washed up onto the sand.

Lillian doesn't have children. She doesn't need someone coming every week. But she wanted me to come, so I came.

All the time I was cleaning I looked around for the stockings, but I didn't find them. I found other things. There were maybe twelve boxes of tissues in the closet in the hall. Four tubes of toothpaste under the sink in the bathroom. Seven tiny bottles of eyedrops in a drawer. She says her eyes stick. Sometimes when she talks to you, she puts her fingers under her eyes and pulls down the skin.

The next week when I got to the house, Lillian wasn't home. She left the key for me in the mailbox.

I was cleaning the kitchen, the last room before I went home. I saw a note with my name on it on the refrigerator. There were no words there. Does she think I'm stupid, I can't learn to read English? I thought. She knows I go to school to learn.

Instead she drew a pair of stockings.

I was very angry. I knew right away what she was thinking.

Lillian is as big as a barn. Her stockings are a size forty. What would I do with these stockings? I'm a very small size, and also I don't wear stockings. They aren't comfortable to have something covering your legs like that, like an extra skin. But when I saw this note I was afraid. She's going to talk about me to people. Maybe call the police.

I went straight home to my apartment. I didn't stop, even to buy some milk for Shyla. I went into the bedroom to the closet and took down the fishbowl from the shelf. I had to bring a chair from the other room to reach it.

I sat on the bed and emptied the money onto the blanket.

When I first came to this country, I got thirty dollars for a house. But then someone started giving me forty, so I told the other women now I'm getting forty dollars. So they gave me forty. Except one woman. She said forty dollars? I might as well have a live-in maid. So I quit. Other women thought I'm worth forty. Some even gave extra for the bus or a bonus for Christmas.

I work hard for my money. It's all honest money. If I'm cleaning and I find a nickel or a quarter I put it on the dresser. You can check me anytime. I know what can happen to bad money. My father's girlfriend Juana had lots of money. Fat gold rings on every finger, even her thumbs. My mother used to say that's bad money, you'll see what will happen. And she was right. Juana doesn't have it anymore. The last time I saw her, at my father's funeral, she had no jewelry, no fancy clothes, nothing. She looked very old. She's just eight years older than me, but she looked maybe fifty.

I always knew how much money I had. I never told anyone where I keep it. I put a hat over the fishbowl to hide it. I knew I had seven hundred and forty-eight dollars in there.

But when I counted it, there was only seven hundred.

How can it be only seven hundred? I looked around on

the floor by the bed. I counted again, and again. I kept thinking if I count one more time the money will be there.

I called Eddie on his beeper. That beeper is supposed to be
only for emergencies, like if someone's faucet is leaking and
there's a flood in their apartment, they can call him and he'll
come. Or if the heat is broken in the winter. He's very good in
an emergency. Other things it can take him forever. The drain
in my bathtub is clogged and he keeps saying he'll fix it, but
he forgets, or else he gets busy with other things. When I
take a shower in there, the water fills up almost to my knees.
But if it's an emergency he's there right away. When I had the
wasps' nest, he fixed it in a minute.

He called back in three minutes. What is it? Is it the
baby? Not the baby.

No, I said. I'm missing some money.

That's all? he said. Hell, Gloria.

It's a lot of money. Almost fifty dollars.

Maybe you made a mistake.

No. I don't make mistakes with my money.

You're not perfect, he said.

I knew he was talking about Ricky. That I can't do something with him.

I think he took it, I said, very soft.

That wouldn't surprise me, he said.

We were quiet. Then he said, I'm busy here. Why did you
call me?

I don't know, I said.

Are you going to do something about it?

Yes, I said.

What are you going to do?

I don't know. First there's something else I have to do.

I hung up the phone and took fifty dollars from the fish-bowl. I got on the bus and went back to Lillian's house. It was already dark.

When she opened the door, she was wearing a pink and white bathrobe. You can see how big she is. Her legs have no ankles. I could never wear those stockings.

Gloria. Her face was very surprised. What can I do for you? Did you forget something here?

Here, I said, holding out the money. Here is fifty dollars.

I don't understand, she said, pulling the skin under her eyes.

I didn't take your stockings, I said. But here is the money.

I pushed it into her hand. She just stood there with two fingers under her eyes. I saw little pink and blue veins in the eyeball.

Oh, I said. And also I quit.

I started to go.

Wait, she said. Wait, I'm sure we can work this out.

I looked back. The doorway was like a frame of light against the dark. Behind her, I could see the hall stretching away into bright rooms. Everything about these rooms I know. I could clean this house with my eyes closed.

I didn't want to give her my fifty dollars. I didn't want to lose this job. I'm not so rich. All the money I get is something. But I have some pride. I won't have people saying things about Gloria.

I started walking again down the driveway, with my shoulders very straight. Gloria, wait. Her voice came after me. This time I didn't turn back.

I sat on the bus. It was full but very quiet. Nobody said anything, except one man who sat in the front seat rocking back and forth. Let 'em off, let the people off, he sang softly to himself.

Even though it was almost spring, it was cold. Last night it snowed. People still carried winter on them. They stared straight ahead out of their hats and scarves and secret lives. Where are all of them going? I thought. The crazy man. And the woman over there with the face like a bird. What's waiting for her when she gets home? Maybe she has an old mother in a wheelchair. Maybe a son who's blind. Maybe nobody. She lives by herself and eats only milk and toast.

I was angry at Lillian. I was hoping she would get a new woman to clean and the new one would steal all her jewelry and she would never get it back. It doesn't matter, Gloria, I thought. There's other houses you can clean. Because back then I thought if I tell people I have an opening, they'll be calling the apartment all day and all night. They always need someone to clean. And people like me. They like what I do. I'll have to say stop calling already, it's only one opening and I'm only one person.

It didn't happen that way. I never got someone to fill Lillian's day. And then last week Brenda called to say she got someone else.

It's just more convenient, she said. The girl lives right here. And she doesn't have children, so it's easier for her to come on time and what have you.

Okay, I said.

You understand, don't you? she said.

I told her yes, I understand. I was glad about it. I don't

need to have a headache all the time from her stupid vacuum.

On the bus I stopped being angry at Lillian and started to be angry at Ricky. If it wasn't for him I wouldn't have a problem. Because he eats so much, I need a lot more money when he's here. I bought him clothes, I gave him money for his birthday. I can't afford to give away fifty dollars for some stockings.

And he took my other forty-eight dollars. I know in my heart that he took it.

I thought of him coming into my room when I'm not at home. He looks in my drawers first, because he thinks maybe that's where I keep the money. But I wouldn't keep it there. That's the first place they look. It's just my underwear and clothes and the Bible Jackie gave me that I read on Saturdays. Sometimes I have some chocolates in there. I like the chocolates with the surprise inside. At night before I went to bed I eat one piece. I hold it in my hand, trying to guess is it a nut or a cherry or a cream. I wish right now I had one of those chocolates.

Then he looks in the closet. I have a few things hanging there, not too much. Two dresses and some shirts. I don't buy too much for myself. If there's a sale at the Kmart maybe I buy a few things, maybe some panties so I don't have to do laundry that week. But that's all.

He could see what's on the shelf, no problem. He wouldn't need a chair. So he sees a hat. It's a man's hat. Brown with a wide brim, something like my father used to wear to church. I took it from Eddie because he never wears it, and I thought this is perfect to hide the fishbowl. Then underneath he finds the bowl. I used to keep the money in an empty Coca-Cola bottle, but the opening is very small. It's easy to push the money in but hard to get it out again. With the fishbowl it's easy. He reaches in his hand and takes out some money.

He wouldn't take it all. If he takes it all, it's easier for me to miss it.

But what does he think, I won't miss forty-eight dollars? Some women maybe. If he had a different mother. There's a woman where I clean who has checks in her drawer she forgets to cash. From five months ago, six months. I told her you have money in there, *mucho* money, and she laughed and said yes, yes, aren't I terrible? But I am not this way.

I felt the anger inside me like a stone. I will find that money.

Ricky wasn't home when I came to the apartment. I went to his room. I never go in there. I couldn't remember the last time I came in. I always keep the curtain closed so I won't have to see anything. I don't want to know. But now I moved it away and stepped inside.

The room was a mess. All over the floor was food, clothes, comic books, games for the Nintendo. If I would come to a house like this, I'd say no, thank you, I can't do something here. I won't clean this for a hundred dollars.

I started to look through his things. I found two more cigarettes. I found a note from his teacher he's failing math. I never saw that note before. There was a place for me to sign. But I didn't find the money. There was a quarter and a penny on the floor near the bed and that was all. It must be he already spent it.

The stone inside me grew bigger and bigger. I couldn't hold it anymore.

His black bag was under the bed. I took it out and started to put things in it. I packed up what he had, what he wore. I put in the three new shirts and all the Nintendo. I didn't want to see anything in this apartment that belongs to Ricky. I started to leave the room, but then I saw the poster of the red sports car on the wall over the cot. It was big and bright. The headlights were like white eyes, laughing at me. With one hand I reached across and pulled it down. It made a loud ripping sound. I tore it in half. In half again. My fingers felt good tearing the paper. I thought I can feel every little bone and muscle in there. I left the pieces on the bed, scraps of red and white.

Then I zipped up his bag and carried it to the hall outside the apartment. I didn't care where he went.

Later Eddie called on the phone. Did you find the money?

No, I said.

Do you want me to do something? I'll make him sorry he ever came here.

No. I'll do it.

He was quiet for a minute. Then he said, Okay. So should I come up?

I don't think tonight, I said. I'm too tired.

Come on, *querida*. It's been a long time. *Mi amor.*

I don't feel like it.

I heard him breathing into the phone. I could feel his breath in my ear.

What is it? I said.

He's changing you, Gloria. You're not the same as you used to be.

What are you saying?

I don't know. Something's missing. I'm just not excited anymore, you know?

Suddenly I was sick and afraid. I wasn't expecting this.

Some things I liked about Eddie, some things I didn't like. I didn't like when I had to stay home from work because Shyla was sick and he wouldn't watch her. I didn't like when he kissed me and pushed his tongue into my mouth and his tongue was big and hard and tasted like meat. I didn't like when he cut his nails and left the dead pieces in the bathroom sink so they floated up when I ran the water.

But I liked his thick arms, his square hands. I liked the way he rubbed my shoulders. I liked how on the anniversary of the day I moved into my apartment he came up again wearing a brown paper bag. Surprise, he said, and he gave me a dozen red roses from under the bag. And it was funny all over again.

I liked him to be there at night, even if we didn't say anything.

He doesn't mean it, I thought. He wants to scare you.

But the sickness stayed with me. I'm throwing him out, I whispered into the phone.

It's winter out there, Eddie said.

I don't care. Let him find someplace to go.

There's places for kids like him, he said. I've been telling you all along. In the army they get them up at four in the morning to do push-ups. They don't have time to get into trouble.

I took a shower. The tub filled up with cloudy water. The top of the water had a thin layer of soap. I lay down in it. I touched my body under the water.

When I was a child we used to take a bath and put baking soda in the water. It was for the mosquito bites. The water burps and bubbles like something alive. It comes up under your skin and takes away the itching. But when you get out of the tub it starts again. If you scratch it, it bleeds. I always had scabs on my arms and legs from scratching.

People used to ask me about it. They said Gloria, you look like you were through a war. My teacher asked me.

It's just the mosquitoes, I said.

Is that all? You have some cuts and bruises.

No, I said. That's all.

She looked at me until I looked away. Try not to scratch, she said. Sit on your hands.

I started to keep my hands underneath my desk.

Something was bothering me, but I couldn't say what. Something with Ricky. It was there in the corner of my mind, waiting for me to find it.

•　　•　　•

I moved deeper into the water. If you make a circle with your thumb and finger and dip it in the soapy water you can see colors there. Pink and green and purples. Then you blow it very gently to make a bubble.

I remember once when Ricky and Miguel were little and I washed them together in the tub for washing clothes. I had time, I was feeling good. And I blew soap bubbles. Perfect, like little worlds. They liked that. Their small fingers reached up to catch them. So then they used to ask me for it. But other days I didn't have time for bubbles. I was busy in the store. When I came home, I was tired. My mother gave them a bath. If not for my mother, they would go dirty for days.

I stayed in the bathtub until the water sank lower than the island of my stomach and the tops of my fingers shrank to little skulls.

Before I went to bed, I put the chain on the door. So even if you have the key you can't get in. I turned off all the lights in the apartment. Then I lay down on the bed and put Shyla on my stomach. She was very nice and warm. Just a little baby. She didn't give me any problem yet.

I couldn't sleep again. I was cold, then I was hot. The heat in the room made a noise like someone breathing. I kept thinking of things I had to do. I have to fix the closet door. It is coming off the track, and it could fall down anytime and hurt the baby. I'll get up now and fix it, I thought. But then I forgot and I was thinking other things. Something was still bothering me.

I must have fallen asleep. Shadows were reaching for me, long thin arms with giant hands. All of a sudden there was a lot of noise. First I thought it was upstairs. I could see the man hitting his wife with a chair. She was crying, covering her head with her hands. But then I realized it wasn't upstairs. It was right here. Open the door! Ricky was shouting in Spanish and in English.

I lay not moving. I didn't care where he went. Let him go to one of his friends.

Open the fucking door! He was banging it with his fist, maybe kicking also. The chain rattled.

I put the pillow over my head. I didn't want to hear it.

It was a long time. Maybe a minute, maybe an hour. I

thought he'll break down the door. He'll wake the neighbors. Someone will call the police. I got up, opened the chain, and let him in.

He stood right inside the door. I didn't turn on the light. He was just a dark shape, holding his bag in his hand. I was so angry I was afraid to open my mouth. I thought if I open my mouth I'll start to cry from anger.

Why do you come back here if you hate it so much? I said finally. Nobody's keeping you.

Fuck you, he said. He started to walk past me. I stood in front of him. He was big, but I didn't move out of the way.

Go, I said. My voice was stronger now. I pointed at the door. Why don't you go? I made it easy for you.

He looked at me. I couldn't see his face, but I saw his eyes shining in the dark. He hated me.

Don't you know? he said. I have no place else to go.

All of a sudden I knew what it was, what was hiding in my mind. Ricky was in my room. He took my money. What else did he take? Maybe he looked under the bed. Maybe he found the gun.

Now I wasn't angry. I was afraid. My hands started to shake.

He took a step. His bag knocked against his leg. Did I hear something inside there?

Please God, don't let him do something, I prayed.

I stood still and let him pass. He went behind the curtain to his room.

I ran back to my room and looked under the bed. The gun was still there, where I left it in the leather case. There was a thin layer of gray dust over it. Nobody touched it.

Everything broke inside me. I sat down on the edge of the bed and cried.

• • •

I didn't go to sleep. I sat all night in the dark bedroom. I couldn't get up. I couldn't move.

In the morning I went to his room. He was sleeping. He looked like any other boy, lying there against the pillow. How can he sleep? I thought. My head felt like a hundred little men were running around inside there. My eyes were so puffy they were almost closed. I wanted to scratch my nails across his sleeping face.

I turned on the lamp and held it over him, so the light shone in his eyes.

I want it back, I said.

I don't know what you're talking about, he said. He put his arm over his face to block the light.

Yes, you know, I said. The money.

I didn't take it. Maybe Eddie took it.

Don't be ridiculous, I said.

He sat up.

Maybe he used it to buy film. To take pictures of his fucking rice.

Shut up, I said. I want it back.

I don't have it, he said.

For a small second I thought what if he's telling the truth? Maybe this one time I did make a mistake. Maybe it was someone else. In this building people take things. Once the boy from downstairs took the screws from Shyla's baby carriage. I came down and the parts were loose and later I saw him outside playing with a pile of screws. I needed them for my dump truck, he said. He is not all right. The doctor bumped his head when he was born, and there's something wrong with his mind. So I just took back the screws and fixed the carriage.

Then Christmastime Jackie left me a basket of fruit in the hall outside my door, and it disappeared. She called to see if I got it. What basket? I said. I didn't see a basket.

They were such nice pears, she said. And oranges.

Another neighbor brought it back. She said she saw some kids from the second floor on the stairs carrying a basket and when she came they dropped it. The fruits rolled down the steps. Some of them had damage, but some were still good. The oranges you could eat.

But this time was different. Nobody can get inside my apartment. I have the two locks and the chain. It had to be him.

His sneakers were next to the bed. Very huge sneakers.

I was dizzy. The light I was holding shook back and forth, making crazy patterns on his face and on the walls. His face changed from a boy's to a man's to that of some kind of wild animal, waiting to jump up and tear me apart.

I took a step back. The lamp fell from my hand and crashed on the floor. Shit, Ricky said, sitting up in the bed. He raised his hand. To block the light, or something else? I turned and ran from the room.

CHAPTER

18

It was a Sunday at the beginning of summer. I came home from picking up Shyla, and there was a police officer waiting at the door. He had Ricky with him. Finally, I thought. Finally they come to take him. He will be off my hands. I felt something inside me, like a palm leaf opening.

He looked at me. You live here?

Sí.

You his sister? He nodded at Ricky.

Mother.

He looked at me some more, up and down. I knew what he was thinking. You're not old enough to be his mother, to have a boy fourteen. I had shorts and a ponytail. My arms, my chest, they say I look like a kid.

You understand English, lady? he said. He was very fat. The skin on his neck fell down over his collar. His belt pulled into his stomach, cutting him into two halves like a loaf of bread.

What's the trouble? I said.

Your boy's making trouble, he said. He stole a Nintendo.

He was talking very loud, like he thought that would be easier for me to understand.

I'm not deaf, I said.

I didn't steal nothing, Ricky said.

Other boys saw him do it.

It's a lie, Ricky said. I bought that Nintendo with real money. I didn't steal nothing.

What money? I said. I don't give you money.

After he took my forty-eight dollars, I bought a metal box with a lock and I put my money in there. I wore the key around my neck on a string. When I was working, I felt it under my shirt, hitting gently against my chest. I didn't give him any money. I paid for the breakfast and lunch at school and change for the bus and that was all.

She don't give me nothing, Ricky said to the officer. He twisted a piece of clay in his hands. He rolled it into a perfect ball and then crushed it to nothing, rolled it and crushed it. It made me crazy to watch him.

Don't call me she, I said. How many times do I have to tell you?

I was waiting for the officer to take him away. But he just stood there. I thought maybe he's waiting for me to give permission.

Take him to jail, I said to him. You can take him.

I didn't look at Ricky.

Well, he said. I didn't say jail. This time is just a warning.

No. I mean it. It's okay. I give him to you.

He shook his head. But you're gonna pay for that

Nintendo. He pointed his finger at Ricky. Hundred thirty dollars.

Jesus. I sucked up my breath.

I don't got a hundred dollars, Ricky said. She don't give me nothing.

I don't care about your private life. I'm here to collect the money.

He turned to me. Lady, I need one hundred thirty dollars.

I didn't understand what he was telling me. Aren't you going to take him? I said.

He shook his head. Look, I don't have all day here. If you're his mother, you pay up. That's how it works. Maybe next time you'll keep him out of trouble.

He took out a dirty handkerchief and wiped his face. There was sweat coming down his skin like rivers. Fat people are always hotter than other people.

My body was like a pot, filled to the top with boiling water. I wanted to kick him hard, where it would really hurt. Instead I said, So you don't have kids?

He looked surprised. What's that got to do with anything? he said.

If you had kids you wouldn't say this. You'd know something—

Don't tell me about kids, he said. I grew up with ten brothers and sisters.

Forget it, I said. Then I switched to Spanish. I told him in Spanish exactly what I thought of him. Fat pig.

I don't do Spanish, he said.

I guessed this. If I thought he understood me, I wouldn't say it. Who knows what he can do to me?

Will you get the money or do I have to help you?

I went into my bedroom and opened the money box. I took out six twenties and a ten.

Here. I smoothed it out, very careful, and gave it to the officer. One hundred and thirty dollars. Three houses and some extra.

He took the money. It disappeared somewhere into his clothes. He took the Nintendo also. But Ricky had other Nintendos.

You keep an eye on that boy, he said. If I catch him up to something like this again, I really will take him to jail.

I watched him walk away down the hall. He walked with his legs very far apart.

After he left I said to Ricky, I don't want to see you. I'm going out. I took the baby and left the apartment.

I walked up and down the streets. I wasn't thinking where I was going. When I came to a corner, I decided whether I would turn there or not. It was the time of day when it isn't light and it isn't dark. There weren't too many people outside. They were home with their family, thinking what to make for supper. In some apartments you could see the windows lit up and the people moving behind them. I like to look inside there at what they're doing, standing by the sink or sitting at the table. I like to imagine what their life is like.

I came to a movie theater. I hardly ever go to the movies. They talk too fast, I don't understand the English. And if it's crowded I won't go. But now I went inside. I stood in front of the ticket counter.

I need a ticket, I said to the boy there. He looked to be

about Ricky's age, maybe older. He had bad skin. His face had spots and holes like a sponge.

Which movie? he said.

I looked at the white letters on the list behind him. That one. I pointed.

It's not playing for another hour and a quarter, he said.

What movie is now? I said.

He said a name.

Okay, I said.

He looked at Shyla. I'm not supposed to let her in there, he said. They make too much noise.

I'll keep her quiet, I said.

He shrugged. It's not too crowded. But if she cries, you'll have to take her out.

He gave me a ticket. I knew what he was thinking. What are you doing here anyway? Why aren't you at home cooking supper for your baby? They all think they know something.

The theater was empty. So I didn't have to worry about that. Once I came to a movie with Eddie and there were too many people, so I had to leave. Come on, Eddie said. It's not like we have anything else to do tonight. But I said I can't do it. You can stay if you want to stay. He wasn't happy about it, but he left with me. We went home and watched a movie on TV instead.

But now there were just two old ladies having a very big popcorn and one boy and girl with their arms around each other. Why do they put these damn plastic arms between the seats? the boy said. The girl giggled. I sat in the back row with Shyla on my lap. It was cold. But not a real cold. You could feel that the air wasn't real. When you breathed in, it tasted like plastic. I wished for a sweater.

I used to think who would go to the movies alone. If I passed a theater or a restaurant and I saw a person by themselves, I was very sorry for them. But now it was good. I sat in the dark and let the movie take away everything. It was violent. I like that. A lot of action. I don't like movies you sit there one or two hours and nothing happens. I can sit in my own house for this. I don't need to pay six-fifty.

The voices moved around me. You don't need too much English to understand this movie. I saw from the beginning the girl was going to die. But she didn't see it. People never see their own things.

Shyla made a noise. I put my hand over her mouth. You can't do that, I said. She made another noise. One of the old ladies turned around. I said shut up. I put my knuckle in her mouth, pressed it there against her tongue. She stayed quiet.

The girl died. The man who tried to save her died. I stayed sitting while the white names came up on the screen, until the lights went on and someone came to sweep the popcorn under the old ladies' seats.

When I came out of the theater, it was night. I was surprised. In the movie I forgot that time was passing. I forgot there's a world outside that doesn't stop when it comes to an end. It keeps going on and on and you have to go with it.

● ● ●

When I came home, I called my mother in Costa Rica.
Why did you send him here? I said.
I told you, she said.
You didn't tell me anything.
She was quiet.

Are you still there? I said. I need to know.

It was the goose, she said.

I thought it was a mistake.

Goose? I said. What goose?

I don't know, she said. I wasn't there.

Mama, what are you talking about? Weren't where?

The goose was dead. They said he threw stones at it to kill it.

Who said?

The neighbor. I told them he wouldn't do that. I told them he helps me move my furniture. But I don't know.

Then what happened? I said.

They were angry. They left the goose on my porch.

A goose. I didn't know if I should laugh or cry.

I'm an old woman. I'm too old for this.

She said something else I couldn't hear. What did you say? Mama, you need to talk louder.

Nothing, she said. There was a lot of blood. I scrubbed the porch with soap, and it still didn't come clean.

After I talked to my mother, I talked to Miguel. He doesn't talk so loud. I pressed the phone close to my ear to hear him.

What did you do today? I said.

Nothing, he said.

I could imagine the TV going over there. I knew he was watching it, not paying attention to me on the phone.

I remember when Ricky was maybe five years old and he said he saw color on that TV. You can't see color, I told him. It's black and white.

The leaves are green, he said.

You just think you see green, I said. Because you know that's the color.

No, he said. I see green leaves.

He was getting angry. His face folded and his hands closed to hard little fists, like little hammers. I saw he was going to shout or cry.

Okay, okay, I said, very fast. It's green.

Maybe then I should have thought something. A child who gets angry like that. Miguel didn't get angry. He didn't shout. He was always the quiet one.

Talk to me, I said to him now. Tell me something.

What?

You tell me. Do you miss your brother?

No.

Do you miss me?

I don't know.

There was static. Okay, I said. Well, this phone is not so good. Help your grandma. Do good in school.

Do you want to talk to her again?

No, I said. I'm finished talking.

I said good-bye and hung up.

Even with the lights on, the color in the apartment was gray. Everything suddenly looked very old. The kitchen faucet with its twisted knobs, the torn couch, the ugly fan-light on the ceiling. It's a big round light, like a yellow globe, with the arms of the fan spreading out around it. It makes me think of a giant spider up there. There's a string you pull to turn it on. But only the light part works. The fan never worked.

I leaned back against the wall. I also felt gray and old.

CHAPTER

19

This is when I got the idea to send Ricky away to California.

I am the youngest. I have three brothers. Two of them are still in Costa Rica. They're farmers like my father. But Carlos came to this country almost ten years ago. He has a good job. He has a wife and two kids. They're good kids, very smart. They go to school and get all A's. The little girl sings in the church. I'm not jealous of Carlos. He deserves this. He was always my favorite brother.

We used to collect stones on the beach. The beach is very white and there's broken shells and pieces of coral. Sometimes you see a turtle shell. But we were looking for wishing stones. These are special stones with white veins through them. If you find one you're very lucky. The number of veins tells you the number of wishes you can have. But there's one thing. For the wish to come true you have to give up the stone. You have to throw it away into the ocean.

It was always hard for me to throw away the stone. I wanted to keep it. I rubbed it against my cheek and it felt smooth and cool, and I put it in my mouth to make it shine. Carlos was the one who made me throw it.

What good's a stone? he said.

But it's so pretty.

Pretty is nothing. You have to look what it can do for you.

Carlos is smart. In life you can't just think about what you like now or what you don't like. Something can seem good, but later it will turn bad. Or the other way. It seems bad now, but it's good for you in the end. I always stood a long time holding the stone, but finally I threw it. The circles spread wider and wider until they held the whole ocean. Then the water was flat again, like there never was a wave or a stone or a wish.

I'd ask Carlos to tell me what he wished, but he wouldn't tell. It's between me and the ocean, he said.

When Carlos first came here, he used to deliver pizza. He worked at night and then in the morning he went to school to be an electrician. You have to work very hard and take a lot of tests. But Carlos always had a good memory. When we were younger, I used to wake up very early to study, but Carlos didn't need to study. He heard it, saw it, remembered it. So to become an electrician it took him two years, but he finished what he had to do. He got his license, and he got a job with a company that pays him good money. He has a green card. In my family you know how to work.

The last time I saw him was at my father's funeral. It was a few months before I left Costa Rica to come here. Carlos flew back from California.

I remember he came up behind me at the house and touched my arm.

Little sister, he said. I forgot how tiny you are. You're like a ten-year-old boy.

I leaned against him. His body is hard and solid like a barrel. He smelled spicy, like sweat and earth. All the men on the farm used to smell like that. My father too. It was not an American smell. In California I know Carlos must smell of different things. Metal and grease and a new life. But when he came back to Costa Rica he took again the smell of the land.

But tough, he said. You always were the tough one.

It was strange to be back in my father's house, where I hadn't been for ten years. My oldest brother, Manny, still lives there with his wife. I walked through the rooms, touching things. I picked up a glass horse from my father's collection. He had forty horses in rows along a shelf. When I used to clean the house, I was always afraid to drop one of those horses. Once I did drop it, a blue horse with a wild mane. The foot broke. I was afraid to tell him. I crawled around on the floor, looking for the little hoof, praying please God, don't let him come in here. Then I felt it cut into my knee. There was a tiny drop of blood. I got some glue and put it together, very carefully. I washed the spot of blood off the carpet. I don't think he ever knew. He never said anything about it.

Now I looked for that blue horse. It was still there. I picked it up and touched the crack. I did a good job, you can hardly notice anything. I blew some dust off it and put it back.

I stood in front of the wall with the guns. I didn't touch them. I couldn't make myself touch them.

The room where I slept was off the kitchen. If you lay in

bed there, you could hear the broken noise from the old re-frigerator. The room was all white. White walls, white bed, everything. It was just big enough in there for the bed and a table. They were still there, exactly the same, like nobody went into the room all the time I was gone. Like he was wait-ing for me to come back. He knew I'd come.

His body was laid out in the dining room. I looked at him only once. He had a small gold cross on a chain around his neck. His face was older, with more lines around the eyes and mouth, but it was the same face. Dark and strong. I didn't need to look again. I can never forget my father's face.

There were a lot of people at the funeral. After they buried him, everyone went back to the house to eat. There were long tables filled with food. Juana prepared it. She moved back and forth from the tables in a long black shawl. My mother was also there. It was the only time she was ever in the house. Coming over in the jeep, she held on to the seat and stared out the window, looking for a raccoon or a wild pig or a jaguar that could run out into the road. I don't know why I'm doing this, she said, like she had some choice. She was still married to him. He sent her money. Over there they don't believe in divorce. She stood in the back of the room. Someone gave her a plate of food, but she just held it in her hands without looking at it.

I don't remember too much about my parents living to-gether. My mother got up very early and made coffee and brought it to him in the bedroom. When I got out of the bed that I shared with Carlos, he was already gone. He came home late, after dark.

Then there was shouting behind closed doors. The children will come with me. Children belong to the father. A crash. A crying voice. She must have done something very bad. My father came out in the hall and swung his fist against the wall. Someone pulled me away.

When he talked about her later he always said *your mother*. The wall had a dark bruise.

My father's friends were telling stories. Do you remember the time there was an earthquake and he stayed three hours in the barn to calm down the horses?

He always took care of his animals.

Kids too. The kids always looked perfect when you saw them. Nice clothes, shoes. He raised them himself.

Good kids. They turned out good.

I looked around the room for my brothers. Manny and Luis were leaning against the wall, eating and talking. When he saw me looking, Manny picked up his hand. I didn't see Carlos.

Then he was standing by my elbow. You want to go for a walk? he asked me. I need to get some air.

Yes, I said. The air in the room was fat with too many bodies.

It was warm in the yard. Two dogs were sleeping in the grass. They weren't Arsenio. Arsenio was dead. Juana said he died in the middle of the night, once when my father was away from the farm. She woke up in the morning and he was fallen over on his side by my father's bed, with his legs sticking straight out, like four legs of a table. Juana said she carried him outside and when my father came home he buried him in the yard. He cried while he dug the hole. I tried to think did I ever see my father cry.

How about Juana? Carlos said. She looks so old.

I know it, I said. I couldn't believe it was her. I remembered how she moved into our house, slowly. First her clothes came. Then the painted combs for her hair. Then one morning I came in to make the breakfast and she was kneeling by the stove, trying to light the fire. That's my job, I said, and I pushed her away. I tried to imagine her picking up Arsenio's cold body, but I couldn't. When I knew her, she wouldn't even touch a beetle. If she saw one in the house, she put a cup over it and waited for my father to come in from the farm and kill it. If I saw it, I used to pick it up myself. I walked past her, wherever she was, carrying it alive in my open palm.

Look at the rock, I said to Carlos. I used to think it was so big. You bent over in the grass and it rose up in front of you like a wall. Now I saw it was just a middle-sized rock. I sat down there. Carlos stood next to me. An iguana sat in the shadow, very still.

Over our heads a clothesline stretched from the house. Sheets waved back and forth in the wind like white flags. Carlos leaned back his head to watch them.

That's something I miss, he said. The way the sheets smell when you take them in from outside. In America they use a dryer.

I think I will come to America, I said.

He looked down at me. You're not serious, he said.

Yes, I am.

But you have the boys here, he said.

They can stay with Mama. They'll be fine with Mama.

Listen, Gloria, he said. It's not easy. For a man, it's different.

I'm tough. Didn't you just say I'm tough?

He shook his head. I closed my eyes and breathed in the smell of the grass and the heat and of being a child. The sun was a warm hand on my cheek.

Do you remember when you saved my life? he said suddenly.

My heart turned over. No, I said. I didn't know what he was talking about.

You did, Carlos said. He was chasing me. He was going to kill me, but you stopped him.

I don't think so.

Yes. He reached for me and I screamed and you ran between his legs and he lost his balance. It was here, by this rock.

I never did that, I said. You're remembering wrong.

I remember everything, he said.

It's not true, I said. He was making me angry. He couldn't just make up things about me that weren't true and say them.

You don't want to remember, he said.

I got up from the rock. The iguana ran away into the grass. I started to walk back to the house.

I used to wish he was dead, Carlos said softly.

I stopped.

Yes, he said to my back. All those stones we threw into the sea.

I stood still for a little minute, not turning around, not saying anything. Then I started walking again. He didn't come after me. From the window, I saw him standing by the rock, staring at the place in the grass where the iguana disappeared. After that, I didn't see him anymore alone. If I passed by a room and he was there, I didn't go inside. The next day he left on a plane to go back to California.

• • •

I don't know why he said those things. I didn't ask him about it. I didn't ask what he wished. When I was younger I wanted to know, but not anymore. Now I didn't want to know.

I'm not a hero. I never saved his life.

After I moved to New Jersey, he called to ask do I want to come visit. But I said no. I was busy getting jobs. Wherever they offered me a job, I took it. I even worked Sundays and holidays. If she had a party on Christmas or Thanksgiving and she wanted me to come help, I did that. I cleaned the house, maybe helped her serve the food. Other women don't like to work on the holiday, but I made more money that way. I was living with some people Carlos knew until I could get a place. They told me you give money to the super, he'll find you something. So that's when I met Eddie.

I got my visa made longer for another six months. At the office they said this is it, after this you have to go back to your country and apply for a working visa. And I told my mother I'd come back. But the time passes by. Six months, a year, two years. You see it in front of you like a long road and you think six months is forever, who knows what can happen in six months. You put it out of your head. But then all of a sudden you look up and the time is gone. You're still here, and you can't think about leaving. I never went back to Costa Rica. There's no reason to go back there.

Carlos kept asking me to come to California.

You'll like it, he said. It's always warm, like home.

We'll see, I said.

But then I got pregnant and I couldn't fly. Carlos said he never heard such a thing, but I said Carlos, you're not a woman. A woman feels these things.

Okay, he said. Whatever you want.

This is just not a good time for it. Maybe some other time I will come.

I never did. But I started thinking maybe Ricky can go. Carlos will know what to do with him. I didn't say anything to anybody. Eddie, Ricky. Because I'd have to ask Carlos first, and I didn't know how to ask it. Will you take my son? I didn't know what he would say.

But a few weeks ago something happened, and I knew I had to send him. I couldn't have him in the house anymore.

It was night, almost nine o'clock. I had to do laundry. I couldn't wait anymore to do it. Already I bought two extra packages of panties.

Shyla was sleeping in the apartment. Ricky was playing with the Nintendo. I never left her alone with him. Eddie didn't want it. So I knew I should wake her up and take her with me. But then she'd cry and I'd have to hold her and it's hard to do laundry when you're holding a baby. Then when I got home, I'd have to put her to sleep again. She'd be very tired, and she'd cry some more and not sleep.

I was tired. I had a headache that reached like the branches of a tree down my neck and into my arms. I didn't want to stay up all night with the baby.

I wouldn't be gone a long time. The washer is twenty-six minutes for five quarters. The dryer is however long you want it, one dime for ten minutes. In less than two hours I could be back at home. Shyla would still be sleeping on my bed.

I put the clothes in the cart and took the soap. I got my bag of quarters and dimes. Then I went to stand in front of Ricky.

I have to go out, I said.

He moved his head.

Shyla's here, I said. She's sleeping.

He looked at me fast and then looked back at the screen. I felt an arrow of fear, but I pushed it away.

If the building burns down, don't forget to take her with you, I said. I gave a little laugh. Ricky didn't laugh.

The whole time at the laundromat I was thinking about Shyla and Ricky in the apartment. Eddie would be angry if he knew. If anything ever happens to that baby, I'll kill him, he said. I swear, I'll shoot him myself.

I don't care, I thought. Eddie's not the one who'll have to sit up with her. When she cried at night he made a noise, turned over, and went back to sleep. Then I walked up and down, up and down the bedroom. It was hot. Sometimes I took off my clothes and walked naked in my skin. Outside the traffic was loud and angry. You could hear cats howling. Finally maybe she'd fall asleep. I'd put her down. She'd wake up and cry again. I was so tired I couldn't feel my body. I would think to myself why did I have this baby? Why do people have children? I'd hate Eddie, hate Shyla, hate myself.

Or there was a siren. The police station is not too far from the apartment, and if there's a siren at night, Shyla always wakes up. One night there were three sirens, one after the other. Every time she fell asleep another one started, until I thought I can't stand it anymore. I picked up the phone and called the station. I can't believe you have so many emergencies, I said. How are people supposed to sleep?

We're just doing our job, ma'am, he said.

What can you say to that? I slammed down the phone.

The first washing machine I took didn't work. I put the quarters in, but then when I pushed Mixed Colors nothing happened. So I had to move all the clothes to a different machine. I didn't get my quarters back. I tried to get them. I hit the machine with my hand. I kicked it a little bit. Shit, shit, shit, I said. A woman folding towels stared at me. But the quarters were gone.

I sat on one of the blue plastic chairs across from the machines. Usually I like the way the laundromat smells. All the different soaps. But now I didn't like it. It made my head hurt worse. I tried to do some homework for school. I opened the book and tried to read what it said there. The words were like little ants on the page. I couldn't read it.

I stared out the glass front of the laundromat at the painting on the building across the street. They painted a whole side with boys playing basketball, so the kids won't write things there. I passed it every day and I never thought about it. But that night I saw there's something wrong with the picture. The bodies are too long and thin, and the heads are too small. They look like skeletons. The lights from the street made the colors too bright. Blues, greens, very bright whites.

Someone was shot last year outside this laundromat. They never found the murderer. Eddie started asking again are you carrying the pepper spray. I'm carrying it, I told him, and some nights I did.

The washing machines made a lot of noise. Sometimes they moved a little bit on the floor and knocked into each other.

What if a noise wakes her up? I thought. Maybe she's already up.

I went to the phone to call. But I'd used all my quarters, because of the broken machine.

Excuse me, *señora,* I said to the woman with the towels. She had a little girl with her. You have a quarter?

Sorry, she said.

I knew she was lying. I saw she had some in a roll under the towels. But I didn't say anything. What's the point? There's some people just don't ever do something nice for another person. I went back to my chair.

The girl was playing cards. She put them on the chairs. A line of clubs, a line of hearts. If someone wanted to sit there, they couldn't. But there was no one. I watched her play. Some people say you can see the future that way. I had a great-aunt who read cards. When you went to visit her in her house, she spread them out across the table in her kitchen. I remember once when I was a child I went there with my mother. She lived two houses down the street. Her kitchen was dark and had a funny smell, like some kind of medicine. The cards were old, yellow where they should be white, and bent at the corners.

This king means you'll meet a wonderful man who will kidnap you and take you away, my aunt said.

Zoraida, my mother said. Don't fill her head with this nonsense.

No, tell me, I said. I want to know.

I leaned against the table. The faces on the cards stared back at me, kings and princes, magic people from magic lands.

Zoraida laughed. You see, little mama? she said to my mother. This one will go far.

The girl saw me watching her. She got up and whispered something to her mother and they both looked at me. I turned my head to the street again. I tried not to look at the skeletons playing basketball, but I couldn't stop looking at them. Like when you see a dead cat in a puddle of blood on the road, with its head crushed and flies on its eyes, and you don't want to look but your eyes go there anyway.

I saw Shyla lying on the floor. Ricky was stepping on her, on her face, her hands. There was blood spreading out around her. Stop it, Gloria, I told myself. Just stop it.

The time moved very slowly. I put my clothes in the dryer and put in four dimes for forty minutes. I looked at the verbs some more. I said to myself I won't look at my watch until I finish three pages. When I finished, I thought it must be half an hour. I looked. It was only ten minutes. Then when I looked again it was twelve minutes. After fifteen minutes I took out the clothes. They were still wet. I piled them into my cart and went outside.

He has a knife, I thought. I bought him a knife with a white handle.

And there's a gun in the apartment.

I ran all the way home. When I crossed the street I forgot to look, and the man in the car stuck his finger up and yelled something. I didn't care. I just wanted to get home. I ran up the steps to my apartment. The cart bumped behind me.

Ricky was not on the couch where I left him. Ricky? I shouted. Ricardo!

I had to see Shyla. The bedroom door was still closed. I ran to open it.

Then Ricky was standing in front of me. What the hell, he said.

I stopped.

What's going on? he said.

Nothing, I said. Nothing.

Everything looked the same. There were some dirty dishes in the sink, but that was all. I bent over to rub my legs. Already I could feel the bruises there.

So how did it go?

Ricky walked past me to the couch.

I opened the door to the bedroom. Shyla was asleep. Her cheeks were pink, with little lines from the sheet. I leaned down to hear her breathing.

Thank you, Jesus, I whispered.

The clothes were wet and heavy. I had to put them someplace. I got a pile of hangers and started hanging clothes all around the apartment. T-shirts in the bathroom. My bras in the bedroom. Shirts and shorts from the door-knobs.

I saw Ricky watching me. The dryer was broken, I said. He didn't say anything.

You could help, I said.

I held out a hanger.

I'm going out, he said. I'm meeting some people.

He got up and left the apartment.

When he was gone, I stood looking around the room.

The clothes were hanging like parts of broken people. Tops in one place. Legs in another place. Everything all mixed up.

I fell down onto a chair. My heart was making a hole in my chest. And I knew I couldn't keep him there anymore. I am breaking to pieces. I am going crazy.

21

Once when I was fifteen, sixteen, I was very sick. I was working very hard in my father's house, not eating or sleeping. My father didn't notice. Nobody noticed. That girl, Gloria, she has lots of energy, they said. But inside I was falling apart.

I made mistakes. I lost things, a pair of scissors, money for groceries. I cut my thumb with a knife, too deep for blood. I leaned too close to the stove, so the fire jumped out and caught my hair. The ends curled up and fell away. There was a horrible sweet smell. What is it? my father asked. I said a mosquito flew into the fire. Later I cut off the burnt ends and threw them out in the yard. I cried a little, not for my hair but for myself and what was happening to me.

One day I stepped in front of a jeep. The wheels crunched on the rocks, so close I could feel the fire of the rubber against the dirt. Afterward I stood in the road, shaking. It wasn't because he almost hit me. It was because I didn't see or hear him coming. I didn't feel him like you usually feel a jeep, a little earthquake in the ground under your feet. When I was a child, if I heard a jeep I ran out to the road to watch it pass. I waved. Not too many cars went by there.

I started to see things. I would see people missing an arm or a leg. Manny came into the kitchen where I was cooking and I screamed Jesus, what happened to you? Because I thought he had only one arm. He looked at me like I was crazy. I closed my eyes and when I opened them again things were in their place. Manny had two arms. Are you all right? he asked. I laughed. Of course, I said. I was only joking.

Or sometimes I saw spots of green or red light, spinning around my head.

I dreamed I was dancing. I twirled faster and faster and the skin fell away from my body and the blood poured off me, and I was thinner and thinner until finally I disappeared.

Then one day I fainted. Carlos found me.

I'm fine. I tried to sit up. Let me get up. I have to work.

No, he said, holding me there.

He told my father.

What is it? my father said. Are you in trouble? If you got yourself in trouble, girl, I swear I'll kill you.

No, I said. It's nothing. I'm fine, I can work. I swear, I said, but he made me see a doctor in town, to make sure it wasn't that. The doctor said I needed a rest. I went to stay with my mother until I could get strong again.

He's killing you, she said. Why didn't I see? Those marks on your hands. And look how thin you got.

She was sitting in a chair, soaking her feet in a tub of hot water. She looked up at me, and there were tears in her eyes.

No, Mama, it's okay, I said, but she shook her head. I am a bad mama to you, she whispered. She rubbed her knee, moving her hand over it in little circles. I stared down at her feet. Under the water, they were ugly and strange.

She had trouble with her legs. They were swollen, and her left knee was bad. But she still did all the work in the house. She woke up early to cook the meals. She liked to finish all the cooking by noon, so she could go out and visit the relatives. Even before I woke up, the smells were there. I had the clean smell of rice in my dreams. Or sometimes I woke up and the house smelled warm and sweet and I knew there was *batata* baking in the oven. It's a Spanish potato. The outside is not so pretty, purple with black bruises, but when you break it open the inside is hot and sweet. My father used to eat it. Whatever else he was eating, he liked to have a *batata*. In my country they say the skin of the *batata* is good for the digestion. I was always careful to make sure he had one. If there wasn't enough, I gave to him first.

All morning in my mother's house there were black beans jumping up and down in a giant pot on the fire. The steam made a white cloud over the stove.

She worked from six o'clock until noon. She swept and polished the floor. She pushed away the furniture to clean underneath. Once a week, on Saturday, she took down all the curtains to wash them in the yard. Her neck and shoulders shone with sweat, like dark glass.

She wouldn't let me help her. You rest, she said. I drank sleep like it was honey and I couldn't have enough of it. When I was awake, I sat on a chair in the sun and my mother brought me fruit juice and bowls of small, sweet bananas.

There's a juice they make from *cas* that tastes something like pineapple. I always liked it. While I was sick, she kept big pitchers of this sweet juice in the refrigerator. Have another glass, she said. Sugar gives strength.

I watched her on the floor, sewing blankets. She crawled back and forth to pin the seams. She moved her left leg with her hand.

Your knee is supposed to carry you, she said. I have to carry my knee.

She talked to me about the different cousins. This one's getting married. This one's getting rich.

I let her words pass over me. I didn't know these cousins too well, because I didn't grow up together with them in the town.

Sometimes in the middle of working she'd look at me and the tears would be there again, like rain waiting to fall. I pretended not to see. I didn't know what to say to my mother crying. I don't want someone crying about me. I can take care of myself. I am strong. It was my father made me strong.

When I was better, I went back to his house. When you live somewhere, that's how it is, you always go back. I wasn't sorry to go. I couldn't sit all day and watch my mother work. That is not a life. My father needed me there. He sent my brothers all the time to see when I was coming home. He was a good father to me.

• • •

Only later, when I was eighteen and I was pregnant with Ricky, did I move in again with my mother. I stayed there and I had my baby and I got the job in a store. First the old man wasn't sure about me.

In your voice I find that you are not very big, he said, turning to me. His blind eyes were the color of milk.

Yes, I said.

I can't tell you too much what to do. You're on your own. Can you handle that?

For a minute I stood without answering. I never worked before like this, I didn't know what needs to be done to run a store. But then I remembered what my father told me the night he taught me how to dance. You can always do something. When the time comes I will know what to do, I thought.

I can do it, I said.

Well, I have no one else, he said. We will try it and see.

I kept the books with the money. I carried the heavy boxes from the back of the store. When I finished one thing I started another one, and he never had to tell me anything. He never had one thing to complain about me. I worked there all the years.

In my mother's house I slept on the sofa bed, where I slept with Carlos when we were little children and the whole family lived together in the town. At night I opened it, and in the morning I closed it up again. That's how it had to be. Because I couldn't stay in my father's house then anymore.

CHAPTER
22

I called Carlos. There was an answering machine. I hate to talk to a machine. I didn't leave a message. Then in a little while the phone rang. It was him.

Gloria, he said. Did you call?

How did you know?

I just had a feeling. I know you. Anyone else would leave a message.

I told him about Ricky. He's crazy, I said. Do you know, he killed a goose.

When I was his age, I hung the chickens on the clothesline, Carlos said. It rained and they went in the mud and got dirty and I was afraid he'd be angry at me. So I washed them and hung them up to dry.

He's not dangerous, I said. He wouldn't hurt anyone. A goose isn't a person.

Most of them died, he said. There were feathers all over the ground. Did you forget that also? That's why he was chasing me. He wanted to kill me because I killed his chickens.

All of a sudden I remembered white feathers, like a hundred pillows exploded in the yard. I stood there and my hands were shaking and all I could think was this must be how the world looks in places where the cold comes. This is snow.

You can't do it by yourself, Carlos said. He needs a man. What happened to that guy you're with?

Eddie hates Ricky, I told him. Ricky hates him also.

Do you want me to take him for a while? He can deliver pizza.

My voice was trapped like a butterfly in my throat. I couldn't say yes. I couldn't say thank you. Finally I said he likes pizza.

Carlos laughed, and I laughed too. It felt good. When's the last time I laughed like that? I thought. I couldn't remember.

One day Eddie came into the bedroom with a toilet plunger stuck to his head.

Like my hat? he said. He stood in front of me and turned all the way around, like a good horse they're showing to sell.

I stared at him. What are you doing?

He stopped turning. Nothing. Trying to make you laugh, I guess. Remember? Ha, ha?

It's not funny, I said. A toilet plunger isn't funny.

Nothing's funny anymore, is it? he said. He didn't wait for me to answer. He left the room and I watched him go.

I'm losing him, I thought. I'm losing everything.

When can I send Ricky? I asked Carlos on the phone.

Right away, he said.

I hung up and told Ricky you're going to my brother.

One more chance, he said.

No.

He looked at me like I am nothing. I am not nothing.

• • •

When I came home from the airport, I saw the cut he made in the couch. You could see from the threads that he used a very sharp knife.

You see that, Eddie said. He has a knife. He's dangerous.

He bent down to look at the cut. Probably a switchblade, he said. I wonder where he got it.

I didn't say anything.

You're lucky he never knew you had the gun, Eddie said. Just think what he could do.

I had in my mind to sew up the cushion, but I was always very busy. The stuffing is coming out of the hole. When you sit there, little pieces stick to your clothes, like feathers, or snow.

CHAPTER

23

After Ricky went to California, I was happy but I was not happy. I was happy because now there was no more Ricky, no more trouble. I came home from work and the apartment was empty and clean how I left it. There were no dirty dishes in the sink for me to wash. No ants. But I was not happy because I didn't know what he was doing over there. I didn't know if he was making trouble.

Eddie was only happy. He bought a Japanese cookbook and cooked something Japanese. Seaweed or something like that. I always wanted to try this, he said.

Yuck, I said, but he just laughed.

I brought you some chocolates, he said.

He worked a lot in the basement. When he came up to my apartment there were splinters in his fingers and pieces of sawdust in his hair. It's nothing, he said when I saw the splinters. But I said you can't just leave them there. I boiled a needle and poked it into his skin to get them out. It wasn't easy.

The skin on his hands was thick and hard. I held his wrist very tight in my hand. That hurts, he said.

Don't be a baby, I said.

Then one day he said come downstairs. I want to show you something.

I don't go too much to the basement. It's Eddie's place. It's dark with fat pipes running up and down the walls and all kinds of tanks and switches. Once the lights went out in the apartment and Eddie wasn't home and when I called him he said go downstairs to the circuit breaker and turn these switches. But I was afraid to touch them in case I turned the wrong one and the whole building would blow up. So I came back upstairs. I stayed in the dark until Eddie got home.

I told you the third switch on the right, he said.

I just wasn't sure, I said.

The basement smells like old rain and the wood Eddie keeps there. He has wood all different sizes and shapes piled up in the corners and leaning against the walls. There's some other things down there. Somebody's broken bicycle. A small refrigerator where he keeps some beer. A crib from a baby who lived here once. Eddie said the baby died in her sleep and the family moved away and left the crib. He didn't know what to do with it so he brought it down to the basement. It's a fine crib, he said. Maybe someday somebody'll use it. But he never said we'll let Shyla sleep there.

So here it is, he said. The toy box.

It was even bigger than I thought. Eddie stood looking at it with proud eyes. He had a can of beer.

I went around to the stores to see how they make them, he said. I saw they all have doors that open up and down. And I thought to myself that's no good. It can fall on her fingers. So I did it this way. See, the door slides across. Try it.

I put my finger in the little hole and slid open the door. Inside was a big dark hole, waiting to be filled with toys.

Eddie watched me. He took a long drink and wiped his mouth with his hand.

Do you like it? he said. You didn't say if you like it.

I like it. It's perfect.

I have an idea, he said suddenly. Let's plan a vacation.

Vacation? Where?

You'll see. I know of a place.

He kissed me on the mouth. He tasted sweet and sour from the beer, and it was not a bad taste.

The place was called Happy Days Ranch. Eddie showed me pictures of the fields where we can go riding and the lake where you swim and the craft barn where you can paint a pot. They give you the paints and little brushes. You do it how you like to do it, not how someone tells you. I never made something like that. The only thing I painted was when I helped Eddie with the apartment, and we used only white paint that stuck in our hair like glue. When I saw the picture, I told Eddie I want to do a pot.

You can do a pot, he said. Whatever you like.

At night they have music and dancing. Are you a good dancer? he said.

I can dance.

Cha-cha-cha, he said, grabbing me.

Happy Days is a place for families. There's all kinds of things for the children. A sandbox and swings and a room with colored plastic balls. Shyla will love it, Eddie said. She's a lucky baby. I never had a vacation until I was in my twenties.

I smiled. Let's take her picture on a little pony, I said.

All week we talked about the vacation. I started to get excited about it. At night I sat on the couch together with Eddie and looked at the pictures in the brochure. The rooms had waterbeds. You can lie down and dream of something and the waves will carry you back there. I will send Jackie a postcard. Eddie was talking about making a reservation.

I talked to Carlos only once that week. I didn't call him. He called me.

Ricky starts work tomorrow, he said. They give him a bicycle for deliveries.

That's good, I said. That's very good.

I didn't even know if Ricky could ride a bicycle. Did he have a bicycle in Costa Rica? It's not your problem, I told myself.

Do you want to talk to him? Carlos asked.

I don't know, I said. Does he want to talk?

I'm sure he does.

I heard Carlos put down the phone. He called Ricky's name. There were words I couldn't hear.

Then someone picked up the phone. I thought it was Ricky. I felt nervous. Why are you nervous? I thought. He's over there in California.

But it was Carlos again. No, he said. He doesn't want to talk.

It's okay, I said, taking a breath. I'll call you in a few days.

I hung up the phone and came to sit by Eddie on the couch. He put his arm behind me along the back of the couch, so his fingers touched my shoulder.

You see, he said. Sometimes you have a good idea. That was a good idea, to send him to your brother.

Yes, I said. I was quiet.

What are you thinking? Eddie said.

Nothing.

I stared down at his bare feet stretched in front of him. He cut his toenails like a letter "V." I never saw toenails like that. I always wondered about it but I never asked. I don't know why. I thought maybe now I'll ask him.

You have to be thinking something. Tell me.

Why does he hate me? I said.

It just came out of me.

I don't know, Eddie said. Because you brought him here. Because you left him there. There's a million reasons kids hate their parents. Anyway, you know he's crazy.

We were quiet.

I used to hate my mother, he said. It was when she got older. I'd go to visit her at the house, and she'd forget who I was. She called me Ernie. My brother's name. I told you, all the kids in our family have names that start with *E*. I hated her for mixing me up with him. Because my brother never visited her once. He left Puerto Rico, and he never even called. He could be dead.

He turned to me. You must have hated your mother sometimes. Or your father, since you lived with him.

Until then I had never told Eddie too much about my parents. He didn't ask a lot of questions. But now I answered right away. I didn't have to think about it. No, I said. I never hated him.

You must have. You just don't remember.

I shook my head. You can't say that. You don't know.

He shrugged. Okay. Maybe you were a different kind of kid. Or maybe you had a better life.

When I was a child, I used to lie in bed at night and think what would it be like if my father was dead. But it was only thinking. I couldn't believe it really. My mother, I could imagine how it would be if I didn't have a mother. My life would still be my life. But my father, no. In my heart I always believed I would die before he would. Because I couldn't see it any other way. I didn't want it another way.

It was Carlos, not me. Carlos who said he used to wish he was dead.

I never hated him, I said again.

I hear you, Eddie said.

•   •   •

I remember when he went away. It was for business. He took my brothers and Juana and left me alone in the house. First I thought it will be nice, I will have the whole house quiet for myself. I can wake up when I want to wake up, I can eat when I want to eat. I will cook only vegetables, no meat, and eat it outside on the grass under the stars. But one day passed and another day. The house was big and quiet, and the quiet was like a wool blanket pressed against my face. I started to worry what if they aren't coming back.

I thought maybe I should go to my mother, but I knew if he came back and I was gone he would be very angry. He needed me there to watch the house. He trusted me to do that.

One night, the third night, I couldn't sleep. I got up and

went into my father's room. I never went in there except to clean. It was a big room, with a very big bed like an island in the middle, and it smelled of the flowery perfume Juana sprayed on her neck and arms to keep cool. Her hair combs were on the table on her side of the bed, like she threw them down without thinking. I like everything to have a place. In my room, in my life. There has to be some order, there has to be rules. But Juana was not like that. Where it falls, it falls. Sometimes I was jealous of her, because if something wasn't right she could just walk away from it. If the cake fell flat in the oven, or if she and Manny or Luis had a fight. They used to fight a lot, because my brothers talked to her like a younger sister, they didn't respect her to be the woman in the house. She would scream and scream, and then in the morning she'd come out from her room smiling like nothing happened. And with the cake, she'd just cut it up and eat it. For me, it is different. It chews away at my heart, and I have to do something to make it right again.

I fixed the combs so they were spread like a neat fan on the table. Then I went to my father's side of the bed. Even though the house was empty, I kept expecting to see him there, in the doorway. But I pulled out the drawer in his table. I found what I wanted.

I picked up the ocarina and carried it to the kitchen. I sat down at the table. I did not make any light. For a long time I held the ocarina in my hand, feeling its warm shape against my palm. My fingers touched the holes.

When I put it to my mouth, it made a soft sound, like the wind. I blew into it, gently first and then harder. I pretended I was giving a concert. There were many, many people and their faces were happy. They smiled and clapped. I sat in the empty house and played the ocarina for those people who wanted to listen. I played until the sun came up. Then I wiped the mouth of the clay with a cloth and put it back where I found it. Later that morning my father came home.

You were gone so long, I said.

He laughed. Did you think I would leave you? he said. You know I'll never leave you. I will always be here.

•   •   •

He was sixty-seven when he died. Manny came to my mother's house before it was light. He stood in the kitchen, like a piece of furniture that didn't belong. It was his heart, he said.

No, I said.

Manny just looked at me.

He was never sick a day in his life. He never even went to the doctor.

That doesn't mean anything, my mother said from the corner. He always had angry blood. That's what killed him.

He knew this was coming, Manny said. Every day last week he had the priest come to the house. He gave thousands of colóns to the church. Father José was with him when he died.

Do you want some coffee? my mother said.

No, Manny said. I have to be getting back there. There's things to do at the house.

After he was gone, I stood on the porch together with my mother and watched the day come. There was a wide open space between us.

So now I'm a true widow, she said. Her voice was flat, with nothing behind it.

I didn't look at her. She didn't look at me. The sky burned with orange clouds, like it never did before or after. Two thoughts were fighting inside me. He can't reach me now. And I should have gone back there. It should have been me who was with him.

In the years after I left my father's house I used to dream about going back there. How will it be if I just show up at the door? I thought. Because I knew he wouldn't come to me. He was the father, I was the child. No matter what happens you're still your father's child.

Sometimes I looked at my mother and I thought who is this woman? I felt nothing for her. Maybe because I wasn't raised there. Maybe it was something else. Those were the times I thought to go back to him. Carlos said don't do it, but it was always in my head. I would be getting ready for bed or working in the store and it would come to me. I will go back there with my son.

I saw in my head how it would be. I would show him the child and say see, he looks like you, and he would feel Ricky's strong arms and legs and say yes, I see, a little man. He would take Ricky's hand and they'd walk together into the fields, and I'd stand in the doorway and watch them go. Then I would move into the house and light the wood stove and cook tortillas, hot for when they came home.

Once when Ricky was five, six years old I decided to go. I dressed him up nice in his blue coat with the four silver buttons and went out to the farm. A neighbor gave us a ride on his cart. Where should I leave you? he asked. I said leave us at the end of the road. We'll walk the rest of the way.

I started walking up the hill. Look, I said to Ricky. You can see the chimney.

Where?

There, behind the hill.

We came to the gate outside the fields. I stood leaning against the old gray wood, staring up at the house. I could feel the splinters of the wood through my shirt.

Good girl, my father would say, looking at me. You did right with him.

Then I heard the gun, far away across the fields.

Ricky jumped away from the fence. I want to go home, he said.

Don't you want to see the house? I said. There's pretty things inside. Carpets.

No, he said.

Your grandpa is waiting to meet you.

I don't want to see him, Ricky said.

I remembered what Carlos told me in the weeks after I ran away.

Don't come back here, he said. You'd be crazy to come. He might hurt you, hurt the boy.

The gun came again. Men shouting. My hands started to shake, and I held one in the other to stop the shaking.

You're right, I said to Ricky. Let's go. I don't know what I was thinking.

Some days later Manny came to the house to see my mother, and he told us how my father had shot a jaguar that kept stealing away his chickens.

Every night another chicken, Manny said. Finally he had enough. He stayed outside all night, waiting. This time when it came he was ready. It's either him or me, he said, and Jesus knows it won't be me.

So that was the gun we heard, I thought. That was all.

The time went on. I knew my father was getting older.

What does he look like now? I thought. The lines on his face. He always had deep lines because of the sun.

Sometimes I thought to write a letter. I smoothed the white paper in front of me. But what would I say? And how would I finish it? Love, Gloria?

There was a voice inside me. It's your job to take care of him. He is your father.

It stayed with me. You are a terrible daughter. But I never went back. I never wrote the letter. I rolled the paper into a ball and threw it away.

25

When Carlos called three days ago to say Ricky was missing, I thought what will I tell my mother when I talk to her? How can you tell your mother you lost your son like you lost your money?

He doesn't have any money. He doesn't know this country. It's not like Costa Rica. Maybe he's hurt someplace. Maybe bleeding. Maybe dead.

I gave birth to that baby, in the back room in my mother's house. Such a big baby. It hurt so bad. I bit down on my lip until the blood ran into my mouth. Scream, my mother said. It's better to scream. She held my head. But I didn't scream. I didn't make even one sound.

Ricky also didn't cry. He was born into the room and the room was quiet. But I knew babies are supposed to cry. To take air in their lungs and start them breathing. So I hit him to make him cry. I was so weak I could hardly sit up in the bed. But I did that. I pulled all my strength into my arm to do it.

Then when I saw his lip that way, I cried and cried. I thought he was going to die. I thought it was a punishment to me. Because I left my father to save my son.

I didn't mean to have a baby. I was young, just eighteen, I was taking care of my father's house. But then something happened.

He was a man who worked on the farm. His name was Ramón. He lived in a hut on the edge of the farm with some of the other men who worked there. He had rabbits, forty, maybe fifty rabbits. There were rows of wooden cages out behind the hut. When he wasn't working on the farm, he was taking care of these rabbits. If I had some time I liked to go look at them. I brought them little scraps left over from the kitchen. Their noses tickled my hand through the bars of the cage.

I didn't mean to have so many, he told me. But rabbits multiply very fast. You start with two and in a few months you have a hundred.

He used to sell them in the marketplace.

One day he gave me a black-and-white rabbit with long ears. I brought it to the house.

Don't bring it inside, my father said. Rabbits smell.

But my father liked that rabbit as much as I did. He fed her vegetables from his hand. She grew big and lazy. You could open the door of the cage and she would sit still and not even try to come out. When I left his house, I didn't worry about the rabbit. I knew my father would take care of her.

I started to go more and more to visit those rabbits. Then one afternoon Ramón took me to the cornfields. It was late, after the workers all went home. The sun was low in the sky. It turned the fields to gold.

Did you ever have raw corn? he said. That's the best way to eat it.

He picked two ears of corn and peeled them. The long corn threads stuck to his bare arms.

I bit into the corn. It exploded sweet in my mouth. No one can find us out here, I thought.

All through the summer I met Ramón in the cornfields. We lay on the ground and ate the corn and the birds came down around us to peck the cobs. I always ate mine in neat rows, pulling each kernel from the cob with my teeth. Ramón was different. He had no order to it. When he finished, his cob was a mess of broken kernels.

Why did I go with him? I don't know why. He was handsome, but it wasn't for that. I didn't care about that. Now when I try to think I can hardly remember. His face is a shadow with other shadows in my memory. But there was a feeling I couldn't explain, like maybe he could give me something. When I was with him, I wanted what I didn't have. If we talked, I wanted more than the words. If we had sex, I wanted more than his body. I kept waiting for something to happen.

When I told him I was pregnant, he left the farm. He didn't tell me he was going. I came into the kitchen with the breakfast and his place at the table was empty.

Ramón had to go suddenly, my father said. His mother is dying in another town. He is a good son to her.

I went to his hut. The room inside was bare. The rabbit cages were empty. Maybe he let them go free. Maybe he killed them. I don't know. I never saw him again.

The next day a new, younger man was in Ramón's place.

When I served the food, I didn't look up from the plates.

I thought I can get rid of the baby. I knew other girls did it. Once I even went out to the barn with a knife, thinking to do it. I boiled the knife first to get it clean. I sat in the cool dark barn for a long time, with the hay poking like sharp fingers into my clothes. It was night. I could smell the horses, warm and alive in their stalls. They made loud breathing sounds deep inside their noses and stamped their feet against the ground. Nobody will ever know, I thought. I wasn't afraid of the pain.

But something inside me kept my hand. I couldn't put a knife to my child.

There was no choice. I knew I would have to tell my father.

• • •

I waited until after supper. He always had a glass of wine. I thought that would be the best time to say it.

His face turned to stone. The black in his eyes closed to little points. He stood up from his chair. His shadow was black and tall and filled the whole room. Slut. I'm going to kill you.

The wineglass crashed to the floor. He reached for me. Hands like tables.

For myself it is okay. It's what makes you strong. But now it was not just myself. There was the baby. I was afraid for the baby.

I screamed. My feet slipped in wine as I ran. The air smelled of sweet red wine.

• • •

Some weeks later Carlos told me what happened that night, after I left. He said my father took a gun and went outside and shot at the trees. He ran back and forth in the dark. I'll kill them, he shouted. I'll kill all of them. In the morning, in the sun, the tree trunks had holes from the bullets.

Will they die? I asked Carlos. Will the trees die?

I don't know, he said. That's not the point.

I need to know.

I am sorry for the trees. I am sorry for hurting my father. And now I think, what do I have for it? What was it for?

What can I do to make it right again?

26

I couldn't sit still. All night I waited for the phone to ring. I walked back and forth from the kitchen to the bedroom. I peeled the nails off my fingers, and when there was no more nail I peeled the skin. Blood soaked into the cracks in my hands and dried there, black.

What's the matter with you? Eddie said.

I had to tell him. Ricky is gone.

So it starts again, he said. The circle starts again.

Where do you think he went? I said.

I don't know. Who knows how he thinks?

Well, one thing I know. He won't come back here.

Why not? Who's going to stop him?

Me, I said. I don't want him here.

Eddie just looked at me. Then he went down to the basement.

He can't come back here, I said.

I'm going on vacation. I'm going to ride a horse and

dance the cha-cha. I'm going to paint a pot with houses and trees and a very big sun.

Yesterday I didn't go to work. I didn't call to tell her I wasn't coming, I just didn't go. It's not like you, Gloria, she said to me later when she called, but I didn't care then. I brought Shyla to the neighbor, then I came back home to the apartment. I sat in a chair and waited for something to happen.

All day I waited. I stared at my hands in front of me on the table. They looked different, a stranger's hands. It got hotter and hotter. Greasy smells came into the apartment from the restaurant down the street.

Every time I heard a noise I thought it was him. I kept thinking the door would open and he'd be standing there. Where were you? I'd say.

Fuck you, he'd say in English.

What will I do if he comes back here? I asked myself. But I pushed it out of my head. He won't come back. He hates it here. Didn't he say that?

I went to the window and looked out on the street. There was a boy in a black T-shirt walking with his head down toward the apartment. He was a big boy. It's not Ricky, I said. But I waited for him to look up, just to be sure.

At noon I thought if I don't go out I will die in here. I went to the supermarket. I went up and down the aisles, taking things off the shelves. Milk, bread, apples, Oreos. I didn't even look what I was putting in the cart. It came to almost a hundred dollars. In my life I never bought so much food. I don't even eat Oreos. I piled the things on the counter in the kitchen, next to Eddie's aloe plant.

Also on the counter, in a dark corner, is the pot with the amaryllis bulb Jackie gave me when I was pregnant. I picked it up and turned it around in my hands. The plant finally bloomed, sometime around Christmas, one red flower like a kind of strange bird. But it only lived a short time. It's supposed to come back next year if you cut the leaves and keep the bulb in a dark place, but I don't think it will. Why would a flower come back here?

Then in the afternoon he called. I will send you money, I said. Go back to Carlos.

I believed he would do that. I wanted to believe it.

• • •

This morning I went to the drugstore. The Western Union has an office there. I know because once Jackie's ex-husband went on a trip and he had everything stolen from him at the airport. They took his bag with his clothes and his wallet and all his money. He didn't know anyone to call except Jackie. She had to send him money. She said what can I do, I can't just leave him there.

The drugstore doesn't open until nine o'clock. I got there early. I stood on the sidewalk with the money in my pocket. I kept my hand on it so nobody could take it from me.

A woman came up to the building and tried to open the door. She had a leather bag and big dark sunglasses and a green kerchief tied around her head. She made a cup with her hands around the glasses and leaned her face against the window. It's not open yet?

What do you think? I said. If it was open, you think I would just stand here?

Well, excuse me, she said. She moved away from me to stand against the building.

I followed her. I'm sorry, I said. My son's in trouble.

Well, that ain't my fault now, is it? she said. She turned away. Then she turned back. What kind of trouble, honey? He in jail?

Not yet, I said. He ran away.

I couldn't see her face behind the glasses.

It's tough, she said. I got a son. How old did you say he is?

Fourteen.

Fourteen, she said. What's he doing running away?

I don't know.

Never mind, she said. Fourteen's young still. He got time.

We stood for a few minutes not saying anything. She took off the glasses and squinted at her watch. They should be open any minute now.

I have to go to work, I said. I clean houses.

That right? she said. I'm not working now. My son's sick and I got to stay home to take care of him. I'm gonna get something for him here.

She made her voice go softer. You don't have to go to the doctor, you know. They'll rob you of everything. Just come here and tell them what's wrong and they'll give you something.

They can do that?

Honey, they can do whatever they want.

I scraped my sneaker against the sidewalk. There's a hole in the toe. I don't know how it got there. I don't remember when it came.

I have some openings, I said. You know someone looking for a cleaning lady?

No, she said.

I do a good job, I said.

She nodded. We were quiet.

Then she said, Don't worry. He'll come back to you.

I shook my head. No, I said.

Sure, she said. They always come back.

You don't understand, I said, but it was nine o'clock and the man was unlocking the doors.

She gave a little wave and went inside.

He can't come back, I said.

I stood on the sidewalk. People passed by and looked at me. A woman with a baby carriage. A man with a shopping cart of empty cans. Across the street a man walked up and down in front of a store, stamping his feet and clapping his hands. He's crazy, I thought. The whole world is crazy, and nobody is doing anything to change it. I couldn't stop watching him.

You waitin' for something, baby? he called to me.

No, I said.

I turned and went into the store.

CHAPTER
27

He stands in the open door. I stand looking at him.

He's a big boy, almost six feet. And I am little. My head doesn't reach even to his shoulder.

But I am strong. I drink milk. You wouldn't guess it because I'm little, I'm thin, but these arms are strong. When I was just a little girl in my father's house, I cooked and cleaned for twenty men. It is my father who made me strong.

I came back, he says again.

Behind him is his black bag, open on the floor. Things spill out of it like the stomach of a dead animal.

I see, I say.

We stand facing each other through the open door of my apartment. His shadow is big against the wall.

I know what he's thinking. You can't do anything. I see it on his face, in his eyes.

I want food, he says. I didn't eat for two days.

He takes a step. His shadow moves to swallow me.

And then I am back there, in my father's living room, in a red dress with a white collar. And I feel his hands on my shoulders and feel the blood running out of my heart and I am lighter than the pieces of gray dust you can see floating in the air. And he looks at me—

I walk into the apartment and past Ricky to the bedroom. I put down my books, lay Shyla on the bed. She is crying again. She is also hungry.

One little minute, I say. Soon Mama will get you some food.

I bend down and reach under the bed. Dust on my fingers. When I come out of the bedroom, Ricky is still standing there.

Is there chicken? he says. And then, what the hell—

He jumps back. He is fast but I am faster. Eddie was right. It's not so difficult.

You point it and shoot.

A scream. Blood like a fountain. The smell of blood.

Move on, like a big elephant.

CHAPTER

28

Outside on the street the siren makes circles of noise, like water when you throw a stone in. Red lights flash on the walls and over the ceiling. I move to the window. The men are running with Ricky to the ambulance. The doors of the ambulance are open, and white light spills out onto the street. There is a police car parked at the curb. People stand in a crowd, watching. Everything is very bright. The night is red and white.

Inside, there are more people crowded in the hall. Jackie and her daughters, and the man from upstairs is here with his wife. She stares at me with big dark eyes through the open door of my apartment. Jackie is holding Shyla.

The police officer leans very close to me, so I can feel his breath. He smells like peanuts and cigars. I know this one, he was here before. He is very fat. He puts the handcuffs up against my cheek.

How could you do it? he says. Do you know what you did?

I look straight into his eyes. I don't move. The metal is cold against my skin.

And then we are outside and he opens the back door to the police car and I get in. There's a metal grate, and I am behind it. We start to drive away from the curb.

Then I see Eddie's old blue truck. He's driving in and out of the traffic like he's drunk. He pulls up in front of the building and jumps out, leaving the motor on. He is waving his hands and shouting. Wait, wait. He runs toward the car. When he moves fast, you can see his limp.

The officer stops the car. Eddie bangs on the window on the driver's side, and the officer opens it.

I got a crazy call, Eddie says. The neighbor said something, somebody is shot—

Who are you? the officer says. Do you know this woman?

Sí. I know her.

She shot her son.

No. He leans against the car. His face is wide and blank.

No, he says again. She wouldn't do it.

I want to laugh. What does Eddie know about me? What did he ever know?

I look out the window. There is a moon. I see it hanging between the buildings at the end of the street, white and beautiful. The same moon I used to watch early in the morning in Costa Rica.

Gloria. Eddie puts his face in the window and twists his neck to see me in the backseat. I look at him through the grate. His face is broken apart into little squares.

You shouldn't drive like that, I say to him. You can get a ticket. They can take away your license.

He looks at me like he never saw me before.

You can't talk to her now, the officer says, rolling up the window. I gotta go.

The car pulls away. Eddie is still standing there. I watch him from the rear window, getting smaller and smaller, until I can't see him anymore. Then I lean back against the seat. My father's face grows out of the dark. Strong, alive. He smiles at me, and I smile back. I hear music, like the wind. He would be proud.